COYOTE

Linda Barnes

COYOTE

A
Carlotta Carlyle
Mystery

Delacorte
Press

Published by
Delacorte Press
Bantam Doubleday Dell Publishing Group, Inc.
666 Fifth Avenue
New York, New York 10103

Plane Wreck at Los Gatos (Deportee) lyrics by Woody Guthrie, music by Martin Hoffman. TRO— © 1961 (renewed) 1963 Ludlow Music, Inc., New York, N.Y. Used by permission.

Love You Like a Man written by Chris Smither. Copyright © 1970 UNITED ART-ISTS MUSIC CO. INC. Rights Assigned to EMI CATALOGUE PARTNERSHIP. All Rights Controlled and Administered by EMI U CATALOG INC. International Copyright Secured. Made in USA. All rights reserved.

Library of Congress Cataloging in Publication Data

Barnes, Linda.
Coyote : a Carlotta Carlyle mystery / Linda Barnes.
    p.   cm.
ISBN 0-385-30012-3
I. Title.
PS3552.A682C6   1990
813'.54—dc20   90-34505
                                                                     CIP

Manufactured in the United States of America

Published simultaneously in Canada

November 1990

10 9 8 7 6 5 4 3 2 1

BVG

For Sam

ACKNOWLEDGMENTS

There comes a time in the development of a manu-
script when the author needs to view it with eyes other
than her own. I'd like to thank Richard Barnes, Susan
Linn, James Morrow, and Karen Motylewski for provid-
ing that critical vision. I'd also like to thank Gladys
Roldan for correcting my fledgling Spanish, and John
Hummel for his contribution.

I am grateful to my agent, Gina Maccoby, for her un-
flagging support, and to my editor, Brian DeFiore, for his
expert judgment.

Sometimes events in life as well as in literature warrant acknowledgment. I extend my deepest appreciation
to Dr. Benjamin Sachs, Dr. Judith R. Wolfberg, Dr. Jo-
hanna Pallotta, and Alexandra Paul-Simon for helping to
make the dedication of this book possible.

Woe to the sheep when the coyote is the judge.

—Folk saying

The crops are all in and the peaches are rott'ning,
The oranges piled in their creosote dumps,
You're flying 'em back to the Mexican border;
To pay all their money to wade back again.

Good-bye to my Juan, good-bye Rosalita,
Adiós, mis amigos, Jesús y María,
You won't have a name when you ride the big airplane,
All they will call you will be deportees.

—From "Deportee"
by Woody Guthrie

1

"A pickle may not remember getting pickled, but that doesn't make it a cucumber."

That's what my mom used to tell me when I was a kid. She reserved it for occasions on which I pleaded forgetfulness, for anything from "Forgot to make my bed" to "Forgot to do my homework." She'd recite it in Yiddish, and I always thought it was a direct quote from her mother, who had heard it in turn from her own mom, my great-grandmother, a formidable woman—a redhead like me—reputedly seven feet tall.

People exaggerate; she was probably no more than my own six-one.

I wanted to repeat the pickle saying to the woman in my office, the one who couldn't remember where she'd acquired my business card. But she wouldn't have understood the Yiddish. As a matter of fact, she wouldn't have understood the English either.

Her name was Manuela Estefan.

She sat in the client's chair by the side of my rolltop desk, her pinched face framed by dark hair. She wore a white blouse with a V-neck, long sleeves, and some kind of embroidery on the collar and cuffs. I'm no needlework expert, but the design didn't have the flattened look of

1

machine stitchery, and I got the idea it might be home-made. With the blouse she wore a dark cotton skirt and black pumps. Her hands were tightly clasped in her lap. She blinked as if she hadn't seen sunlight for days, and I wondered if I should yank the shade on the September sunset.

Her name was one of the few things we'd established. This was because she spoke little English and I spoke little Spanish.

"Car-low-ta," she said, giving the name its Spanish pronunciation, as if she thought I was Hispanic too. I didn't have the Spanish to explain that my Scots-Irish dad had named me for some movie star who made one B film in the late forties and then hit the skids. My ad in the Yellow Pages didn't even mention my first name—what with the still existing prejudice against female private investigators. And, like I said, I hadn't yet learned how Manuela had come by my card.

She'd had it clutched in her hand when she rang the doorbell. She'd shoved it quickly into a plastic handbag, but I'd seen it.

Usually my clients make appointments, but I have nothing against a little walk-in trade. If she didn't mind my shiny face, my jeans and T-shirt attire, and maybe a hint of eau de locker room, I was perfectly happy to take a crack at earning a fee.

I hoped my stomach wouldn't growl too fiercely.

If Manuela had timed her surprise visit any earlier, she'd have been out of luck. An hour ago I'd been in the gym at the Cambridge YWCA, playing possibly the best volleyball of my life. I was still awash in the afterglow, winded, sweaty, loose—and damn proud of an upset victory, another step toward the City League finals, a step nobody thought the Y-Birds could take.

2

We'd started off lackadaisical, losing two games before we found our rhythm. Fortunately, like baseball and life, volleyball has no time limit. You keep on playing the points, whacking the ball, until one side takes three out of five, and a game never ends until one team is up by two points.

At the beginning of the third game I could feel the momentum swing. The rusty gears who'd lost the first two games so awkwardly suddenly meshed as a team and won the next two.

There'd been points that left me tingling. Plays I longed to see again on some nonexistent instant replay screen. Had Kristy, our captain, really made that impossible dig? Had I managed to spike that shot? That hard?

The final game was like floating, like slow-motion choreography, like shared silent prayer. I knew what every other player would do before she did it. Winning that last point didn't mean any more to me than breathing.

I must have talked a mile a minute taking Paolina home. Sometimes a good game affects me like that. Paolina, my little sister—not my real little sister but my Big Sisters little sister—had been curiously silent, moody. I wondered if she resented the Y-Birds, disliked sharing me with the team. I'd have to spend more one-on-one days with my little sister.

I'd made it back to the house in good time, driving like the part-time cabbie I am but managing to avoid a traffic ticket. I'd slipped my key in the lock, patted T. C., my cat, and raced to the kitchen to pour a tall glass of orange juice in preparation for a pig-out dinner.

I was surveying the dismal contents of the fridge when the doorbell rang.

My stomach was getting impatient, not having

3

counted on playing several rounds of twenty questions in Spanglish.

Manuela's eyes flickered and she stood abruptly. I thought she was going to storm out and return with an interpreter. But she only marched as far as my late Aunt Bea's rocking chair and the *Globe* I'd abandoned on its cushion.

I'm better at guessing weight than age, but I figured her for anywhere from seventeen to thirty. Her hair was long enough to brush her shoulders, fine and straight, giving her a dark Alice-in-Wonderland look.

I hadn't read the paper yet. It was still rolled and bound with a rubber band. Some days I read it devotedly; some days it goes to the bottom of the parakeet's cage right after I read the comics.

Manuela grabbed it triumphantly, opened to the Metro section, and spread it on my desk, stabbing one of her bony fingers at an article below the fold. Her nails were short and unpolished, her hands chapped and lined. They made her nearer thirty than seventeen.

I grimaced because the first thing that caught my eye was the front-page picture of a wounded child, shot along with twenty-one others in a California schoolyard. The caption said the gunman had used an AK-47 assault rifle. Just walk into your local gun shop and tell the owner you want to shoot up a playground full of kids. Okay, mister, will that be Visa or MasterCard?

I shifted my gaze to Manuela's pointing finger. It tapped a small item, maybe three inches of print. "Body identified," it said.

I pressed my lips together while I read the brief report. I learned that a female corpse, found some three weeks ago in the Fens, had been tentatively identified by a certain document discovered on the body.

4

The Fens is a meandering Back Bay park surrounding a straggly excuse for a river—sometimes called the Fenway, sometimes the Muddy River. It's an urban oasis, replete with the usual muggings, but dead bodies don't turn up there every day. I was surprised this corpse had gotten so little play in the press.

I read on. The name of the victim was Manuela Estefan.

I stared at the woman in my office.

I reread the last sentence, the last paragraph.

I glanced up. My Manuela Estefan had returned to the chair next to the desk, and was nervously twisting a ring on one finger. It was a filigree silver band, maybe a wedding ring. I noticed that her fingernails were not just short, they were bitten, worried away to tiny half-moons with pads of bulging skin beneath.

"*¿Usted es parienta de ella?*" I asked, hoping I'd come close to saying "Are you related to this woman?"

"*No es su nombre.* No her name," Manuela said, shaking her head vigorously. "We—I think—"

"Did someone else—?"

"No. I think— *Mi tarjeta.* She is —no—she *has* my card. You get my card back for me."

"What card?" I asked. "An identification card? Was yours stolen? *¿Por un ladrón?*" The only reason I remembered the word for "thief" was that Paolina had just come back from Bogotá, where she'd lost her camera to a horde of gamins, abandoned children who'd become experienced *ladrones.* It was a cheap camera. I couldn't remember the word for "stolen." I wished I'd paid more attention to Paolina's attempts to improve my Spanish.

Manuela didn't answer, but I'm pretty sure she understood the question. Undaunted, I tried another one.

"Who is she?" I asked, pointing at the article but getting no response. I tried in Spanish. *"¿Cómo se llama, la mujer?"*

"No sé," Manuela mumbled. I don't know.

While she answered, she twisted her silver ring some more. She wouldn't meet my eyes.

"Manuela, we need to go to the police," I said slowly in careful, if possibly incorrect, Spanish. "I'll go with you and nothing bad will—"

"No," she said immediately. "Police" she understood.

"I'll go with you. I know who to see."

"No," she repeated firmly. *"Usted. Sola."*

"Why? *¿Por qué?"*

"Tell them," she said slowly, feeling for the foreign words. "Tell *policía* she is no Manuela. My card, get it back for me."

"They'll ask me how I know she's not Manuela. *¿Comprende? ¿Cómo yo sé?"*

Manuela bit her lower lip and worried at her ring. "Tell them you know," she insisted.

"You must tell them."

"No es posible."

"You told me."

"La Migra," she whispered, glancing quickly around my combination living room and office, as if agents from the U.S. Immigration and Naturalization Service were ready to spring from behind the worn velvet sofa.

"Shit," I muttered under my breath. "You're illegal."

"I no go back."

I knew too many immigrants, legal and illegal, to disagree with her. Instead I reread the brief news article and ran my tongue over dry lips. "It was brave—*valiente*—for you to come to me," I said very slowly. "Tell me about this other Manuela, the woman they think is you. Tell me her name. *Dígame su nombre."*

I'm not sure if she understood what I said, but suddenly she started to cry, her breath coming in short, jerky sobs. She grabbed at her chest, and her skin got pale and blotchy. She made a motion in the air, like she was clutching a glass, drinking, and she said, *"Por favor, señorita."*

I figured she needed a glass of water, if not something a hell of a lot stronger, so I sped out to the kitchen.

It must have taken me all of thirty seconds, finding a relatively clean glass, running the tap water till it was as clear as Cambridge water gets. I didn't even take time to see if Roz had stocked up on Scotch.

When I got back, she was gone.

I ran out the open front door in time to see a car careen around the corner, a beige clunker with a dented fender and a plate I couldn't make out.

I cursed, went back inside, and drank the stupid glass of water. I'd abandoned it on Aunt Bea's best mahogany end table, and the wet circle it left behind seemed like a reproach. I gave it a swipe with the edge of my shirt, went back into the kitchen, found a raggy old dish towel, and polished the offending mark out of existence.

Then I plunked down in my desk chair and reread the article in the *Globe*.

Massachusetts private detectives are forbidden from meddling in murder cases, unless the case is already sub judice and the PI is working for a lawyer, gathering evidence. But the article didn't mention cause of death. It could, I supposed, have been natural causes, exposure, a lightning bolt for all I knew.

I lifted the *Globe* off the desk and an envelope fell to the floor. Just a white envelope with five hundred-dollar bills inside.

The bills were crisp, folded once in the middle. I smoothed them and counted them again. Manuela hadn't

7

said anything about murder. All she wanted was to get her card, her *tarjeta*, back.

I considered her plastic handbag, her cheap shoes. I wondered what she'd done to earn those brand-new bills. I sat at my desk a long time, fiddling with the cash, watching the sun sink in a flash of crimson, followed by violet and a deepening blue. Then, prompted by my stomach, I went to the refrigerator and whipped together a couple of huge BLTs on toast. I washed them down with enough Pepsi to keep my kidneys afloat.

Also enough to keep me awake for the night.

I tried everything. A long hot soak in the tub, even a meaningless Red Sox game on my flickering black-and-white TV. Finally I hauled my guitar out from under the bed and set about practicing some tricky riffs, hoping some of the magic feeling of the volleyball game would return and inspire my fingers. But the picture of that silver ring on Manuela's work-roughened hands kept edging between me and the blues.

2

"You're absolutely right," Mooney said the next morning at nine through a mouthful of doughnut.

He wasn't talking to me. Lieutenant Joseph Mooney of the Boston Police Department rarely says things like "absolutely right" when he's talking to me. He was addressing the phone, and from the look on his face he'd been murmuring polite little nothings for some time, doing a lot more listening than talking, and not particularly liking what he heard.

He yawned, carefully turning away and covering the receiver with one hand so the listener on the other end couldn't catch the noise. He had a dab of powdered sugar on his chin.

As soon as I'd entered his cubbyhole at Southie's old D Street station, he'd nodded me into a chair and winked. Not really winked. He has this trick where he lowers the eyelid of his left eye. No squint. No wrinkles. It looks like half his face has fallen asleep.

I tapped my chin on the spot corresponding to his powdered sugar. He picked up on it immediately, rubbing his jaw. Mooney and I communicate well, part gesture, part mind reading. It helped a lot when I worked for him.

Mooney's got a good face, sleepy or not. Maybe a little too round, on the big-nosed side, definitely Irish. He used

9

to be my boss when I was a cop. He's still my friend, although it's a complicated relationship. I'm getting so I hate the word *relationship.* There are romantic overtones and undertones, mostly coming from his side. On my side there's a lot of warmth. Not heat. Warmth.

Mooney says I don't know how to love a guy who attracts me as a friend. You know, a guy I enjoy, a guy I like to talk to. And considering my history with men, he may have a workable theory. Who knows? A relationship with Mooney might be okay, in a warm kind of way. But the wild and crazy chemistry's not there. Mooney, who's eight years older than me, nudging forty, says someday I'll grow out of the wild-and-crazy-chemistry stage.

I say, who wants to?

Amid the jumble of printed forms, plastic coffee cups, crumpled papers, pens, and pencils on Mooney's desk sat a newspaper. The *Herald.* I picked it up, although it's not my paper of choice, wondering how they'd handled the Manuela Estefan story.

I found it on page seventeen, well after the important stuff like Norma Nathan's gossip column.

While the *Herald* didn't have anything the *Globe* hadn't run, the tone of the piece was of the breathless, breaking-news variety. There were hints at "sexual mutilation" and a coy reference to a key discovery. The name Manuela Estefan was there.

Sexual mutilation would make it murder.

I wondered if Manuela Estefan was a common name, like Jane Smith.

Mooney grunted at the phone, sandwiching it between chin and shoulder while his hands frisked the desk and finally came up with a full cup of coffee. He must have been hiding it in a drawer. He raised his eyebrows at me, and I helped him wrestle the plastic cover off the cup.

I wondered who was on the phone. The police commissioner? The mayor? A city councillor? Mooney didn't suffer long telephone conversations as a rule.

His office didn't offer much in the way of entertainment beyond the single wooden chair I was sitting on, and its hard seat didn't encourage long visits. I knew where the coffee machine was, but the smell from Mooney's cup was not tempting enough to draw me into the hall. I figured if there were any remaining doughnuts, Mooney would have pointed me in their direction. So I was left with the contemplation of either the *Herald* or Mooney's ugly office, which didn't sport so much as a poster on the cinder-block walls. Maybe he hadn't had a chance to decorate since they'd moved him back to Homicide from his liaison position down at headquarters.

Come to think of it, he didn't have a poster at his place on Berkeley Street either. Not even a plant. Bare desk. Bare walls.

I did a complete one-eighty and discovered a map tacked on the wooden door behind me. A close-up of the Back Bay with three pushpins stuck in fairly close together—red, white, and yellow. I stood up to take a look.

"I'll get on it right away," Mooney promised the telephone, and hung up so quickly that I got the feeling the guy on the other end was still talking.

"Carlotta," Mooney said, shoving back his chair. "Sorry. I can't talk. I've got a meeting downtown. I was trying to convince the bastards I'd be more use here, but—"

"I'll drive you," I said.

"Got the cab?"

"Nah, my car. You can make some flunky cruise you back in a unit."

11

He studied his watch. I don't think Mooney likes my driving.

"Hell," he said. "Sure, why not?"

When we were settled in my red Toyota, seat-belted in and trying to wedge ourselves into an endless stream of traffic, I said, "I hear you got an ID on this Fens corpse."

"That's what they tell me," Mooney said.

"You sure of it?"

"Why should I be sure of it yet, just because the papers are printing it?"

"You working it?" I asked.

"I didn't exactly catch the squeal, but I'm involved."

Like most cops, Mooney doesn't give information away freely.

"Do you know if they have a picture ID," I said casually, "or what?"

"Let me see," he said, and I wondered if the pause was for recall or to stare at me out of the corner of his eye. "I think it's a green card. The victim was an immigrant."

"A green card," I started to protest, "but—"

"But what?" Mooney said when I stopped abruptly.

"So that's a picture, right?" I said.

"Yeah, but from what I understand, once the guy finished with the victim, she didn't look so much like her picture."

"I thought it was—how did the *Herald* put it?—sexual mutilation."

"The brain is the ultimate sexual organ, Carlotta. I keep telling you that."

"Not funny."

"You haven't been doing Homicide for a while, kiddo," he said. "Everything's funny on Homicide."

A green card. That I didn't understand at all. A green card is a permanent resident card, a ticket that entitles the holder to live and work in the U.S. for an unlimited time, a prized possession that can be used to apply for citizenship. Not a privilege granted to illegals.

I have had clients lie to me before.

"Where did the lady come from?" I asked. "You know yet?"

"We got her point of entry. Texas. Probably from someplace in Central America," he said, gripping the door handle while I zoomed by a Buick that seemed afraid to take a tight curve. "Guatemala, El Salvador, maybe. I mean, think of the crap she must have gone through—all that shit down there—and then she goes for a walk through the Fens, and bingo, she's a crime stat."

Mooney winced as I made a sharp right to avoid a Volvo wagon that thought it owned the road. I could have just taken Dorchester Avenue to East Berkeley Street, but I was trying to avoid the late commuter traffic, taking cabbie shortcuts. Mooney didn't seem impressed. Of course I had to cross the Fort Point Channel somewhere, and bridges always get backed up. While we were sitting still, breathing exhaust from a heating-oil truck, I brought up the reason for my visit.

"Mooney," I said. "Something funny happened yesterday."

"Yeah?"

"It makes me think your green card ID may be wrong."

"This I need to hear," he said. "Watch out for that car." It was well worth watching out for, a rust-eaten Plymouth Volare, hogging two lanes.

I gave him Manuela's story, not word for word but pretty complete.

"And she just walked away," he said with a deep sigh.

"Ran is more like it," I said.

13

"I'm going to need a description."

"I'm going to give you one," I promised. "I already wrote it up. I'm cooperating."

"Yeah. How come?"

I ignored that.

"Carlotta, am I going to have to remind you to stay out of homicide investigations?"

A Town Taxi tried to cut me off at the bridge. I refused to make eye contact, kept going, and he backed down. Mooney had his hand on the door handle—ready to jump, I suppose.

"Mooney," I said gently, "you've got a homicide investigation. I don't."

"You're just going to forget about this woman?" he said. "I believe that like I believe in Tinkerbell."

"I didn't say I was gonna forget about her. She hired me to do something. Something maybe you can help me with."

"Aha," Mooney said.

"Oho," I responded. The Town Taxi was sitting on my rear bumper.

"You didn't just drop by to give me indigestion driving like a lunatic?"

"That's an extra," I said. "And I've been driving conservatively, Mooney. If you're in a hurry—"

"Forget it," he said.

"Where do we stand on favors?" I asked.

That wasn't quite fair. He owed me a big one and he knew it.

"What do you think I could help you with?" he said finally. "And watch out for that damn BMW."

"Bimmers can take care of themselves," I shot back. "You think he wants to crease that fancy paint? I thought

14

you might be able to help retrieve my client's green card. She needs it."

"Carlotta, you lose a green card, you go to Immigration and fill out forty-seven forms in triplicate and they give you another one."

"I have a feeling my client doesn't want to go through the process again."

"Shit," Mooney said.

I followed a long line of cars that went through a yellow light at Park Square. I actually thought about stopping, but the Town Taxi behind me didn't. He probably would have driven over me if I had.

"So?" I said. Mooney was looking around for a traffic cop. He could have looked for a long time.

"This meeting shouldn't take too long."

"Where have I heard that before?" I said.

"There'll be a guy from INS there. Afterward we could talk, the three of us."

"How long?"

"An hour, no longer."

I screeched to a halt in front of headquarters. "I'll pick the two of you up here in an hour," I said.

"Absolutely not," Mooney yelled, jumping out at the curb. "Ditch the car. Go buy yourself coffee and a doughnut across the street. We finish early, we'll pick you up there. Otherwise be here, near the steps. Wherever we're going, we'll walk."

"Absolutely not." That's the kind of thing Mooney usually says to me: "Absolutely not."

3

Two hours later I was cooling my butt on the stone front steps of headquarters, watching cops come out, felons go in, and vice versa. I took note of a few undercover narcs and carefully refrained from greeting them even though all the handcuffed punks entering the station seemed to know who they were. I also moved my car in what I was sure would be a vain attempt to fool the downtown meter maids, infamous women who not only ticket you for over-running your meter but actually nail you for refilling the damn thing. These zealous guardians of the public purse make note of every license plate en route, honest to God, and even if you stick in your extortionate quarter per fif-teen lousy minutes, if you stay in one space for over the hour limit, it's a traffic ticket for sure.

I scorn downtown parking lots. They're barely cheaper than tickets. And I guess I enjoy the challenge, the thrill of the chase, the contest between me and the meter maids. I wonder if they get a charge out of ticketing my poor Toyota, wonder if they recognize the car and say: "Aha! Gotcha again!"

Lately the thrill-of-the-chase aspect has come into question, what with fewer legal spaces and more cars competing for each one. Instead of a duel between equals, the traffic-ticket game is starting to feel more like the fox

17

versus the hounds and the hunters. The fox, I think, gets considerably less enjoyment from the chase.

But then he doesn't always get caught. And I like to imagine him back in his den, tail and ears intact, giggling at all those stuffed-shirt red coats and riding breeches.

I'd just made up my mind to stick my car in the cop lot with a scrawled sign declaring it an undercover unit when Mooney saved me from a felony by coming down the steps.

He was followed by a scrawny guy wearing a three-piece suit, dark blue Sears model, and a red tie that might have been described as a power tie on somebody else. On this guy it just drew attention to his bobbing Adam's apple. He had thin brown hair, parted low on the side and scraped across his skull in an attempt to cover his baldness. He clutched a briefcase like he was scared somebody was going to snatch it.

The scrawny guy looked me over when I stood up. I was maybe six inches taller than he was.

"This your source?" he said to Mooney with ill-disguised skepticism. Or definite intent to demean.

"This your INS agent?" I said to Mooney in the same tone.

"Children, children," Mooney said mildly, "let's go have a drink before we start insulting each other. If you'd been at that meeting, you'd need one, too, Carlotta."

So we tagged together through the crowded streets, down Stanhope to a Red Coach Grill that stopped being a Red Coach years ago. I still think of it as the Red Coach, no matter what the neon over the door says.

We grabbed a table near the bar and I got introduced to the Immigration and Naturalization man. He didn't say his name. He didn't offer a handshake. He slid a brown leather folder across the table. I opened it a bit too ostentatiously to suit him. His photo had been taken when he'd had a bit more hair. His name was Walter Jamieson.

"It's *Jameson*," he murmured from across the table. "You don't pronounce the *i*."

I slid my card across the table, placing it facedown, imitating his routine with the folder. He stared at it for a while, and we were spared more hostilities by the waiter, who took our drink orders. I passed, it being slightly before noon. The other two ordered Scotch, Mooney's a double.

"Must have been some meeting," I commented.

"We're not here to talk about that," Jamieson snapped. Then he turned his charm on the waiter. "Bring me a corned beef on rye and hop it. I'm in a hurry here."

Mooney and I exchanged glances. If ever there was a white-bread-and-mayo place, we were in it. I smothered a grin in anticipation of the culinary delights awaiting Jamieson, then I ordered a chicken club; Mooney, a salad.

"The lieutenant said you had some information concerning the identification card found on the deceased," Jamieson said as soon as the waiter was out of earshot.

"You mean, the dead woman?" I said, giving Mooney the eye, as if to say, how could you have brought me this unbelievable clod. The deceased, my ass.

"Carlotta," Mooney said softly while kicking me gently under the table, "why not just tell him what you told me?"

Because he's an obvious idiot is what I felt like saying. Instead I gave him the story, slightly abbreviated. I'd skimped a bit on the tale, even with Mooney, not mentioning the part about my Manuela saying she was illegal. With Mooney, put it down to my normal disinclination to share a client's confidences with a cop. With Jamieson, I figured it would just confuse him.

19

"We'll have to pick up this woman," Jamieson said. "Pronto."

Pronto. He really said that.

"Any chance of getting her green card back?" I asked. "I mean, why should she suffer, just because somebody lifted her card?"

"She can come down to the Federal Building. Here's my number. Have her call, and my secretary will make an appointment."

"Somehow I don't think she'll like the idea of the Federal Building," I said.

"That's the way it's done," he said stiffly. "Of course, she can file a lost card report and go through the usual formalities. I'm offering a shortcut."

"Then there's no way for me, acting as her agent, or for, say, a lawyer in her employ, to get the card back?"

The drinks came. Jamieson checked his watch and demanded his sandwich, which the cowed waiter brought, along with Mooney's salad, even though my order wasn't ready yet. Mooney sipped his Scotch. Jamieson bit deeply into one of the driest-looking bread-and-meat concoctions I ever hope to see and came up talking.

"Are you aware," he said, eyes narrow, tone low, mouth full of stringy corned beef, "of what this sounds like? It sounds to me like some sort of scam to get hold of a green card."

"The murder?" I said incredulously.

He wiggled his index finger in my face. "I mean, your woman reads the story in the newspaper—"

"Never mind that she barely reads English. Neither paper mentions a green card. They say something about an identifying document found on the body. What did she do? Take a lucky guess?"

"You have no idea what these people will do for legal documents."

The man had a shred of something green caught between his two front teeth. I hoped it was lettuce, although why anybody would stick lettuce in a corned beef on rye, I have no idea. I tried another tack. "Can you tell me this? The document you found on the, uh, deceased, is it the genuine article?"

Jamieson glanced at Mooney to see whether I could be trusted with such valuable information. Mooney must have stopped downing his Scotch long enough to give me the okay, because Jamieson nodded his head. He didn't actually say yes. Secret agents might have overheard him.

"So it's genuine and it doesn't belong to the dead woman," I said.

"We're not a hundred percent clear on that," Mooney said slowly. "The way she was cut up, we'll have a hell of a time identifying her."

Jamieson removed a probing index finger from his mouth where he'd been using it instead of a toothpick. "Unless your mystery woman knows who she is."

"My client said she didn't know the dead woman."

"I'd like to ask her myself. Make sure she contacts me before five o'clock today."

"Maybe you weren't listening," I said slowly and distinctly. "I have no idea where my client might be."

"Sure," Jamieson said, gobbling down sandwich moistened by Scotch. "Yeah, but when she calls you, make sure she gets in touch. Otherwise you can get in some pretty serious trouble yourself."

"Mooney," I said, "I am so shaken by this man's threats that I'm going to have a beer. How about you?"

"I'll pass," he said. I called over the waiter and ordered. He assured me my sandwich was on the way. He didn't ask Mr. INS if he wanted anything else.

"Can I see the green card?" I asked.

Mooney opened his mouth, but Jamieson beat him to it. "That would be police property now, Ms. Carlyle. I'd doubt it very much." He had a nasty way of saying *Ms.*

He was going to go on, but the digital watch on his wrist gave a feeble squawk. He shook it and looked perfectly appalled by the time he'd wasted interviewing me. I hope I looked just as appalled. He was exactly the type of guy who'd wear a cheap digital watch with an alarm.

"I have another appointment," he said brusquely, comparing his watch with the clock over the bar while he wrapped a remaining sliver of sandwich in a wadded napkin. "Remember what I said."

"What was that," I asked blandly, "that you said?"

"I want to hear from your client, this Manuela Estefan, within the next few days. Or you could be in some serious trouble." He opened his briefcase furtively, taking care that no one could see the contents, and shoved the napkin-wrapped bundle inside. I wouldn't want anyone to see the inside of my briefcase, either, if all I stored there was leftovers.

"I'm a citizen," I said. "I thought you just made trouble for aliens."

"You don't want to try me," he said. And he grabbed his briefcase and stalked off without reading me my rights.

"Gee, Mooney," I said after a long pause, "thanks so much for introducing me to your friend."

My belated club sandwich arrived. Mooney hadn't touched his salad, so we ate together in companionable silence.

"You want to see the green card?" he said when we

were done, by way of apology for subjecting me to Jamieson.

So we paid up and walked to Berkeley Street. The INS jerk hadn't even left money on the table to cover his lunch.

The card was in a plastic evidence bag. Mooney liberated it for me so I could get a good look. I assumed it had already been dusted for prints.

The more I stared at the card, the more confused I got. The photograph was smaller than a passport shot, slightly blurry. The woman in the photo was shown three-quarter profile, her right ear exposed. She had long, dark hair like my client. Brown eyes like my client. But her face . . . well, there was a definite resemblance, but I couldn't swear to it. If my client had worn her hair behind her ears, I'd have done a better job. Ears are distinctive.

The name on the card was Manuela Estefan. It looked genuine, the INS man had pronounced it genuine, and my client had called herself an illegal alien. I flipped the card over. This was no easy piece of counterfeiting. The front side, the one with the picture, had a white field with pink wavy lines running through it. It also boasted the photograph, an impressive seal in dark blue, and an index fingerprint in a square box. The back of the card was off-white with a beige wave and a white silhouette of the U.S.A. Three rows of numbers.

The card had been laminated. Its edges were rough, as if the job had been done in one of those drugstore machines.

It would have been easier to counterfeit a hundred-dollar bill.

Was my client lying about being illegal? Why?

Was the INS agent lying about the card being genuine?

My fingers played with the edges of the card. I wished I could just pocket the damn thing and give it back to her, case closed. But it wasn't going to be that simple. Not with a woman dead.

Mooney apologized for Jamieson, and I told him he wasn't responsible for all the jerks in the world.

On the way out I asked where they'd found Manuela's card. In a handbag? With any other ID?

"She didn't have a handbag," Mooney said. "Or else the perp snatched it."

"Yeah?"

"Not for publication," he said, "but the card was in her shoe."

"And one more thing: How come you're not absolutely sure about the ID? With the fingerprint and all?"

"Still not for broadcast?" he asked.

"Cross my little heart," I said.

"Victim didn't *have* any prints. He cut off her hands."

4

Driving home, one question bothered me even more than my instant dislike of the INS man.

Why me?

Why had Manuela Estefan picked me to carry her message to the police, to recover her green card? By right of alphabetical order, Acme's got the first ad in the Yellow Pages under Private Investigators. Nor do I have the flashiest ad, although I do indulge my passion for red in bold-face print and a small rectangular outline. Manuela couldn't have decided she'd rather deal with a woman because in the directory I'm just the Carlyle Detective Agency, no gender announced. *Se habla español* is not included in my ad because of laws against false advertising.

Of course. Manuela hadn't needed the Yellow Pages. She'd tucked one of my cards into her handbag.

I don't keep track of my business cards. Who does? But I don't hand them out on street corners either.

The question was who did I know who spoke Spanish and owned a spare Carlyle Detective Agency card. One answer was Paolina.

When I was a policewoman, a lady from the Big Sisters Association came to the station to make a pitch. She said there were hundreds of young girls growing up in the Boston area without successful role models, girls who could use a Big Sister. It made sense to me, the one-on-one approach. I signed up on the spot and was rewarded one month later with Paolina. Paolina's . . . well, she's just what I would have chosen for a little sister. Smart and stubborn from day one, she now alternates between sentimental and tough, weeping over teen romances and arguing with her mom.

She's nearly eleven, and we've been sisters almost four years.

Paolina's mother is Colombian; her father's Puerto Rican. From Daddy she got her U.S. citizenship and not much else. He moved on after fathering a family of four. Marta was two months pregnant when he exited, so he doesn't even know number five exists. Just waltzed out the door one day, leaving Paolina's mother to cope.

Coping used to be what Marta did best. If she hadn't taken ill—rheumatoid arthritis—the family wouldn't be living hand-to-mouth in the Cambridge projects. No way. Marta would be deputy mayor by now, chief liaison with the Hispanic community at least. But she hasn't got the energy anymore, only rare bursts of it when the pain releases her.

Marta keeps an ear to the ground. She hears things even when she's bedridden.

I made an abrupt decision that caused the timid Nissan on my right to honk and screech, zipped across the B.U. Bridge, and headed to Cambridge, convinced that Marta had a hand in Manuela's visit.

Marta and the kids live in the projects near Technology Square. Every year another high-tech high rise comes along to block out their little patch of sunshine. The project buildings aren't bad, red brick two-story houses, four apartments apiece with cement steps and stingy porches. There's a sad-looking playground in the center of the complex, with busted swings and climb-on animals that haven't been painted in years. You can hardly see the gravel for the beer cans.

The basketball court looks better, except the basket rims are bent and the nets are long gone.

I made certain the car doors were locked before leaving the Toyota on a side street. I even set the Chapman lock, something I rarely do. Once, after I'd just had the damn thing installed, I set it, forgot about it, and called AAA to start my car, confirming some lout's opinion about women drivers and embarrassing the hell out of myself. I'd have preferred chaining the car to a tree.

Five black teenage boys were flashing up and down the basketball court, hollering and high-fiving, staying home to practice their slam-dunks instead of going to school, each dreaming of a comfy berth in the NBA.

Marta's doorbell has been out of order for weeks. I keep telling her I'll fix it, and she keeps saying no, the superintendent's required by law to repair it and, by God, she'll hound him till he does. I've met the super, and I figure it's his eternal laziness versus Marta's occasional energy, with the odds in his favor. All he has to do is wait her out.

I made up my mind to bring over a few tools and fix the damn thing next time. Let her think the super did it. He probably wouldn't mind taking the credit.

I banged on the door and yelled her name. I made quite a racket, and nobody so much as looked out a window. Places like that, with heavy daily drug traffic, you keep your windows shut and your curiosity in check.

When Marta finally answered the door, she was using her cane, which meant it was one of her bad days. She hates that cane. The building used to have a system where you could buzz somebody through the door after asking who it was on the intercom. They canned that after thieves stripped the building three times, claiming to be gas men and insurance reps. There was talk of putting in a closed-circuit TV camera, but city officials figured it would get stolen first in any heist. So now the tenants have to eyeball each doorbell pusher through the safety glass and open the door in person.

Marta lives on the second floor, and I felt a stab of guilt at forcing the limping woman down the stairs. The way I grew up, guilt is such a familiar emotion that most of the time I don't even recognize it.

She leaned her cane against the wall and struggled with the lock.

"Carlotta," she said, opening the door and forcing a smile. *"Bienvenida. ¡Pase usted!"*

She was wearing washed-out gingham, a sacklike thing tied with a belt. Marta used to be slim and pretty; now she's wiry and tough. She used to wear makeup and flashy clothes, but lately she hasn't made the effort.

I guess she's given up on catching a decent daddy for the kids.

She can't be much older than I am, but she looks it.

Her cane dropped to the floor and I bent to pick it up. The hallway smelled of urine, laced with disinfectant that hadn't quite done the trick.

I'm never sure how much English Marta comprehends. She's been here a long time, twelve years at least. Sometimes she seems to understand me perfectly. Other times a blank expression closes down her lively eyes, and she declares, *"No entiendo,"* and that's the end of the conversation.

I helped her up the steps, murmuring encouragement and wishes that she would soon feel better. She'd only left her apartment for an instant, but she'd locked all three locks, two of which I'd installed for her. It's that kind of building.

I held her cane while she manipulated two of them. The third popped open, as if by magic, and there was Paolina standing in the doorway.

It's hard for me to describe her features one by one, because they seem to change with her expression. I suppose some people would say her nose is too broad. Her smile more than makes up for it. She's fit and lean, with a boyish behind and long, long legs. No breasts yet. A couple of girls in her class are already starting to bloom.

My mother used to say, *"Kleyne kinder, kopveytik; groyse kinder, hartsveytik":* "Little children, headaches; big children, heartaches."

"Oh," Paolina said when she saw me. "Hi." Then she turned on her heel and stalked into the back room, the one that serves as a bedroom for her and the two youngest brothers. The older boys sleep on a lumpy mattress on the living-room floor. The sofa folds out for Marta.

"Hi," I called after her. I'm used to far more friendly greetings from my little sister. I'm also not used to seeing her home so early on a school day.

"Why didn't Paolina answer the bell?" I asked Marta. "Save you the trek? She sick?"

Marta shrugged and sat heavily on the one decent chair in the room. It was planted four feet in front of a color television, and I got the feeling I'd interrupted a favorite game show. I didn't remember Marta owning a color set. I wondered if it was new.

I sat on the edge of the hide-a-bed. It hadn't been converted back to a couch yet. The bed linens hadn't been straightened. The boys' pillows and blankets were piled at the foot of the mattress.

"Leave it," Marta said, although I hadn't made a move

29

to tidy up. I rarely do; housework and I don't mix. "Just leave it. I'm not the boys' maid. You're not the maid."

"School let out early today?"

"Ask her," Marta said, jerking her head toward the bedroom.

"I will."

"I thought that's why you came. Like the truant officer."

"No."

"She hasn't been going to school. Not even to band practice. I don't know what's her problem—maybe the kids, maybe some teacher—but it's eating at her, and she won't tell me. Maybe she'll tell you."

"I'll try."

She waited, watching a fat lady embrace an utterly sincere TV game-show host who promised a chance at five hundred bucks, hoping I'd go away. I stayed put. "But that is not why you come?" she said reluctantly.

"No."

"Don't sit on the sofa, the lumps'll kill you. Pull over a kitchen chair, no?"

A woman came to me. A short woman with a thin face and nervous hands. A pointed chin, very dark eyes, wide apart. A small nose, a Hispanic woman. A scared woman. A troubled woman. Manuela Estefan. Did you send her to me?

That was what I wanted to say. But I didn't. Marta's devious. She thinks information is a thing to hoard and dole out very slowly and deliberately.

So I started with some chitchat about her recent trip to South America. Five weeks in Bogotá, culminating in the death of Marta's father. I expressed my condolences, although I'd always gotten the feeling that there was no love lost between Marta and her dad. Until the trip I hadn't realized her father was still alive. As far as I could tell, Marta had gone home in quest of an inheritance and returned no better off than before. I assumed the trip had been a failure.

In more ways than one if Paolina, who'd accompanied her, had stopped going to school.

Marta said they'd had a pleasant enough time and her aunts were well and pleased to see their *sobrina,* which I remembered meant "niece."

She spoke mostly in English, with an occasional Spanish word tossed in about the fine weather and the outdoor fairs in Bogotá. The wonderful leather goods. She said that the ice cream was much better than the stuff she remembered eating as a child. Nothing about the drug wars or the bombings that got front-page coverage in the *Globe.*

"The woman you sent to my office yesterday left something I'd like to return," I said, slipping it in casually between descriptions of the exotic flowers you could buy at any corner market, and so cheap too.

Marta kept describing flowers for a while, then slowly ground to a halt. "What woman?" she said, instantly suspicious. *"Una mujer* with no name?"

"Manuela, I think she said."

"I don't know any Manuela," Marta said.

"Manuela Estefan," I said. "I'd like to help her, but I don't know how to find her."

"Maybe she'll find you," Marta suggested, "when she wants to."

"But maybe this woman is in trouble. Maybe if I could find her now, it would save her more trouble," I said.

"Manuela . . . no. I don't think I know a woman with that name," Marta repeated. Her face and voice gave nothing away. She could have been a cardsharp. The most important thing in the world might have been whether or not the fat woman answered the game-show host correctly. She gave the TV her full attention.

I didn't know whether to believe her or not.

"If you should meet such a woman, would you tell her that her green card is safe with a man at INS?"

"La Migra," Marta said, still staring at the TV but spitting out the syllables. "What are they but trouble? Nothing is safe with them."

"I can help Manuela get her card back, but she has to get in touch with me or with a Mr. Jamieson at INS."

Marta considered that for a while. "I don't know any Manuela except the woman who teaches the children at the day-care, and she has a different family name. She is fat and ugly. Yours is fat and ugly?"

I described my Manuela, but Marta kept a poker face.

"Maybe you go now and talk to my Paolina, no?" she said, hitting the remote control so the TV volume increased to a roar. "Maybe to you she listens. To me, no."

5

Paolina's bedroom looked like it had been tossed by thugs. The three single beds, one stretched along each yellow wall, trailed tangled sheets and blankets to the cracked linoleum floor. Underwear, sweaters, and socks were stuffed in and draped over the board-and-cinder-block shelves that substituted for bureau drawers. Nothing was folded. Nothing neatly stacked. The odor of unwashed socks filled the air.

On the plus side, no smell of marijuana.

Paolina's room is usually pretty bad, but today it was worse. It took me a while to realize it wasn't just the smell and the mess. The posters over Paolina's bed were gone, leaving jagged tape marks in the paint. I couldn't remember the missing posters, but they'd been colorful, cheery.

I opened my mouth to remark on the state of the room, took a breath, and thought better of it. Closed my mouth, opened it again, closed it. I was glad Paolina was lying on her bed with her face turned to the wall instead of watching me do my goldfish imitation. I decided not to mention the room. Who needs criticism when they're down? Besides, my own standards of housekeeping are not such that I can hold myself up as a shining example. I don't make my bed either. I mean, why bother? You just have to do it again the next morning.

33

Paolina was in the center bed, the preferred one under the lone window, hers by right as the eldest child.

I made a noise, a polite coughing sound, but she didn't turn her head, so I shoved some junk aside and sat on one of the other beds.

"What this room needs," I said solemnly, "is a parakeet."

They used to put canaries down in the mines, I thought, so the fumes would kill them instead of the miners.

"Huh?" she said.

"Well," I replied, "I had a particular bird in mind. I think Red Emma would brighten things up around here. All that chirping and stuff."

"You tired of Esmeralda?"

"If you're going to call her Esmeralda, she ought to live here. Whoever names the bird gets the bird."

My parakeet—not *my* parakeet, I wouldn't have a parakeet by choice—is a bird of contention. The budgie, originally named Fluffy, for God's sake, belonged to my Aunt Bea and came with the house when I inherited it. Aunt Bea, an awe-inspiring woman in other respects, doted on that bird, and I didn't feel right about getting rid of it. I renamed it Red Emma after a hero of mine and wished it a mercifully short life. It will probably outlive me.

Paolina likes the bird. Since it's undoubtedly green and not red, she has taken to calling it Esmeralda. She's teaching it Spanish.

I opened my mouth to ask her why she wasn't in school. "So how'd you like the volleyball match?" came out instead.

"Okay," she said, her answer muffled by a pillow.

Once, not so very long ago, she would have replayed every point of that final game with me, asking me why I did such-and-such or so-and-so. She's a damned good volleyball player herself.

She was wearing jeans torn at the knees and a T-shirt that her school band had peddled a few years back. MAKE A JOYFUL NOISE, it read in rainbow colors, now faded, with ornamental half and quarter notes in the background. I had a few hiding in the back of my closet. Each kid had been expected to sell a dozen to make money for the band. Those Paolina couldn't sell, I bought.

I'd even given a T-shirt to Roz, my punk-rock tenant, but it was too tame for her and I've never seen her wear it.

She finally sat up and faced me, sitting cross-legged on the bed.

"So?" she said.

"*¿Qué tal?*" I replied.

"*Nada especial,*" she said. It didn't look like "nothing special" was going on. Not with her skipping school and spending the afternoon facedown on the bed. Not answering the door when she knew damn well her mother would have to climb downstairs with her cane.

"*Sábado,*" I said. "I've got another game. You mind coming with me?"

We've been spending Saturday afternoons together forever. We cruise the shopping malls, check out the local music scene, go apple picking in the country. I've taken her to eight Red Sox games, and she really got into it last year. Broke her heart when they didn't make the World Series after pulling off that miraculous twenty-three-game home winning streak. This year she was more cynical, like the old-time fans.

"I don't care," she mumbled. "Whatever you want."

"Hey," I said, "you can do better than that."

"The hell I can," she shot back.

I breathed for a minute. Paolina doesn't talk to me

like that. I have no idea how she talks to her school buddies, but she does not talk like that to me. I figured she wanted a reaction, but I wasn't sure what kind.

I just sat there.

"So aren't you going to ask me why I'm not in school?" she said angrily, throwing a pair of mismatched socks on the floor.

"You want to tell me?" I asked, feeling my way on unfamiliar ground.

"It doesn't make any difference," she said.

"What?" I said.

"Huh?"

"Telling me doesn't make any difference, or going to school doesn't make any difference?"

"Nothing makes any difference, that's all," she said, and she turned her face away so I could study her profile and think about how much older she looked than the girl I'd first met, the one not quite seven years old, with the hand-shaped bruise across her cheek.

"I'm sorry you had to stay in Bogotá so long," I said. "It must have been tough, missing the first days of school. They probably assigned seats and everything, and you're not near your friends—"

"Kids are dumb," she said.

"Did something happen in Bogotá?" I asked.

"Nada," she said. *"Nada especial."*

"But you'd rather stay here than go to school? Is it a teacher?"

"You don't understand," she said, and her sad voice echoed in the tiny room. I could hear myself, age ten, saying the same thing to my mom: *You don't understand. You don't understand.*

"Honey," I said, "I try, but I can't read your mind. You have to tell me."

"Didn't you talk to Marta about me?" she asked bitterly.

Usually she calls Marta Mom.

"Should I?" I asked.

"No."

"Did anything happen to you in Bogotá?"

"Is not telling the truth the same as telling a lie?" she countered.

"Sometimes I suppose it would be, and sometimes not. It would depend on the situation, I guess."

"Oh," she said, turning away from me again and staring out the dirty window.

"Can you tell me what happened?"

"I don't know," she said. "I don't think so."

Great, I thought. No evidence of drugs in the room. Just a kid who used to be open as a sunflower closed as a fist.

"If you didn't come to make me go to school, then why did you come?" she asked.

"Well," I said, "to find out if you or your mom knows a woman named Manuela—"

The door opened and a torrent of Spanish burst out of Marta, so quick that I didn't have a chance to translate half of it. But I got enough. Paolina was not to talk about things that didn't concern her.

She was grounded. She could go to school or she could go nowhere. Maybe it wouldn't be a good thing for her to see me on Saturday.

"Marta," I said, keeping my voice low and calm with an effort, "I need to ask her about this woman, Manuela Estefan. It's a simple question. Maybe it's a teacher at school, somebody she knows."

"Tell her," Marta commanded.

"I don't know anybody like that," Paolina said sullenly. "What's the big deal?"

I apologized for upsetting everybody and left, with none of my questions answered and plenty more bothering me than when I first came in.

6

At seven o'clock that night, fed up with my failure to find
a trace of my client, I decided to do something practical:
earn a few bucks. Manuela's five hundred would not last
forever, and I find I can always use cash, to buy cat food
and size-eleven shoes—which are practically impossible
to find on sale—not to mention paying the taxes on my old
Victorian.

The house is mine, absolutely. Aunt Bea paid off the
thirty-year mortgage eight months before she died. The
only hitch is that the place is so close to Harvard Square,
in such a desirable neighborhood, that property values
shot through the roof. I pay so much in taxes that it might
as well be rent. High rent. I think of it that way and stick
it in the bank monthly so I won't die of shock when the
twice-yearly bills come through.

I prefer to earn the rent as a private detective, but I
still moonlight as a jockey for Green & White Cab Company. I've been doing it for years, ever since I started college. It suits me a whole lot better than waitressing. I like
to drive—it's something you can do while listening to music—and I know the city. Mooney chides me about hacking, says it's dangerous for a woman, as if it weren't dangerous for a man, and as if my cop experience counted

about as much as holding down a desk job with the phone company.

When I was a cop, I got to carry a gun. Cabdrivers are forbidden to carry firearms, but I have yet to meet one who doesn't keep a chunk of lead pipe under the driver's seat.

I've got mine.

Before heading over to G&W, I reviewed my day. After striking out with Marta and Paolina, I'd visited a Cambridge church that provided sanctuary for illegal aliens. Either they'd never heard of Manuela—the one who'd made the paper posthumously or the one who'd visited my office—or they weren't about to say so to any investigator who spoke halting Spanish. Then I'd gotten thumbs-down from a couple of lawyer acquaintances who dealt with immigrants, although one said he'd spread the word that I was looking for the woman. He'd also recommended another place in Cambridge, a legal service agency that helped illegals. Their secretary treated me like an undercover INS agent, which pissed me off.

So I'd gone home to lick my wounds. I consider myself such an obviously trustworthy person that it irritates me when people don't take me at face value. I know that's dumb. Especially coming from an ex-cop who's always telling her little sister not to trust strangers. I guess I have trouble realizing I'm a stranger sometimes.

Hungry as usual, I'd made dinner out of leftovers, chili and Monterey Jack spiced with jalapeño peppers being the main ingredients. Put enough jalapeños in your food and you can't tell its actual age. I fed my cat, who is a far more refined eater than I am, his can of FancyFeast in his ritual spot on the kitchen floor. I even changed the water in Red Emma's cage.

Then I'd phoned in an ad, to both the *Globe* and the

Herald, urgently requesting Manuela Estefan to get in touch with Carlotta Carlyle concerning her card. I decided to run both ads for two weeks: $12.95 at the *Globe,* $8.95 at the *Herald,* where they were having a special. Both of them let me charge it on my Visa.

I'd mailed a third bill to a woman whose runaway daughter I'd retrieved, printing "final notice" in red at the bottom of the page and wondering just what the hell I was going to do if she continued to ignore me. Repossess the daughter?

Roz, my third-floor tenant, housecleaner, and sometime assistant, was upstairs taking her karate lesson. I could tell by the thumps on the floor, and by Lemon's van, which was parked outside. Lemon, Roz's karate instructor, has some three-piece-suit banker's name, Whitfield Arthur Carstairs III, I think, and doubles as a performance artist. They're occasional lovers, although Roz is not the monogamous type, and when their thumping grew more rhythmic, I decided to leave the house for a while.

It's not that I'm horny all the time. As Bonnie Raitt, one of my favorite blueswomen, sings, "I ain't blue, just a little bit lonely for some lovin'." Still, I figured I'd rather drive a cab than listen to Roz's bliss. Roz puts a lot of volume into her lovemaking.

So I yanked a windbreaker over my jeans and T-shirt, and tried to break my speed record for the two-plus miles to G&W. I didn't crack it, but neither did I get caught by the cops.

Instead of picking up a set of car keys and taking off, my usual procedure, I decided to chat with Gloria, G&W's main asset, dispatcher, and co-owner. She sometimes sends me clients, and she just might have referred the lady who'd called herself Manuela.

Gloria motioned me toward her guest chair while she

41

crooned murmuring reassurances into the phone. I sat down, balancing my boom box on my lap. I never like to put anything on the floor in that place. The concrete has the sticky quality of old movie-house floors after fifty years of spilled orange drink and ground-in popcorn.

I always bring a tape deck when I'm going out to pilot a cab. The radios Gloria's got in her old Fords can barely catch the AM top-forty stations, the ones that broadcast at twenty million kilohertz.

My eyes scanned the garage, carefully not lingering in any corners. G&W is ugly but reliable. Nobody ever tries to pretty it up with a poster here or a vase of flowers there. It's too drab to invite that kind of interference. A bright spot would make the rest of the blight unbearable. So, wisely, Gloria does nothing, and the most attractive item in the room remains a square of corkboard with keys hanging on it.

Not that Gloria could do a lot more than organize and order people around, the two things she does best. Gloria operates G&W out of a wheelchair.

"How you doin'?" she asked in her silky voice between phone calls and bites of Milky Way. Gloria eats nonstop and has the bulk to prove it. I have never seen anything nutritious pass her lips.

"One of your cabs is off the road every moment we speak," I reminded her with a grin. "So tell me, you give out my business card to any Hispanic ladies lately?"

"Why? Your ears been tingling or what?"

"Simple question, simple answer, Gloria," I said.

The phone rang, and her hand swooped down on it like a bird of prey. While she soothed an irate customer who'd been waiting two minutes longer than promised, I eyed her desktop.

There was an airmail envelope, addressed to Gloria in

42

a familiar scrawl, lying in the center of the blotter. From Italy. I caught myself before my hand reached out and grabbed it. I glanced up, and Gloria was staring at me.

If I ever blushed, I would have. The letter was from Sam Gianelli, half-owner of G&W. Gloria likes to keep tabs on my love life, and I didn't want her to know how eagerly I awaited Sam's return. Hell, she'd probably tell him all about it.

"I ain't blue, just a little bit lonely . . ." I hoped I'd brought the right tape along. I could hear Raitt's high, fine voice singing in my head.

Gloria hung up, her mellow voice having done its work. "So," she said, carefully not mentioning the envelope, "what Spanish lady? I got a few Spanish-speaking guys working here. I don't remember any of 'em needing a private eye."

"Ever give one of them my card?"

Gloria took another bite of Milky Way. "Nope," she said finally. "What's up? You got a paying job?"

I wouldn't have shaken free without a detailed cross-examination, except that the phones started going crazy. I grabbed some cab keys and left.

A Dodge Aries practically clipped my fender as I drove off the lot.

I ferried conventioneers from their Anthony's Pier Four dinners to their Westin and Marriott hotels, earning enough cash to keep me going at a modest clip for a week. Then I cruised Jamaica Plain, one of Boston's neighborhoods. J.P. has a high-density illegal population, both Irish and Hispanic, with a lot of landlords doing big business renting tiny two-bedroom apartments to ten or so aliens.

I stopped at an all-night grocery store, a mom-and-pop place with Spanish signs in the window. I thought I'd describe my Manuela to the proprietor, but without a picture or a great command of the language, the project seemed silly, so I just bought a can of Pepsi and left, smiling at the guy behind the counter.

A little after midnight that damn white Dodge Aries came by for the third time, parked up the street, and started tailing me. I toyed with him a little while, trying to lead him down one-way streets and into dead-end alleys, but whoever it was knew the city too well to let me backtrack and get behind him.

"INS," I said to myself, turning up the volume on Rory Block's "Gypsy Boy" and helping her out with the scat-singing part. Jamieson, that goddamn INS agent, was trailing me, trying to get a line on Manuela Estefan.

I let him tail me into the North End. It took me two minutes to lose him in its winding maze.

7

By the time I got home—a little past two A.M.—it seemed like weeks had passed since Manuela Estefan's visit. Part of me felt I'd already earned her advance. Hell, I'd earned it just listening to that INS jerk at lunch, not to mention paying for the ads in the *Globe* and the *Herald,* not to mention the gas I'd used traveling to places where I'd earned nothing but *gringa* insults.

Five hundred bucks a day is what I charge my high-toned, Gucci-shoed lawyer clients. I don't have a lot of those. The rest pay on a sliding scale. I go by shoes a lot. I remembered Manuela's worn heels. Five hundred would buy her another day or two.

While making a sandwich—hard salami, Swiss cheese, and fairly suspicious turkey on rye—I checked the refrigerator door for messages. It's our communal bulletin board. Roz is in charge of keeping it neat and tidy, and it will soon qualify for federal disaster funds. She leaves hastily scrawled messages on crumpled scraps of paper under an assortment of magnets, ranging from the plain silver disks I originally bought to the beer cans, horses' asses, and Day-Glo hamburgers she prefers. There were two notes—one from Roz to Roz to buy more peanut butter, the other warning that T. C. was running low on liver and bacon, his preferred flavor of FancyFeast.

I've learned it's wise to cater to T. C.'s culinary whims.

45

I was down to the last bite of my sandwich before I noticed the flashing red light on the answering machine. I punched the buttons that ran the Panasonic through its paces. There was a message from Sam—still in Italy, dammit. He has a wonderfully deep voice even transcontinental phone connections can't screw up. He thought he'd be home in a week, maybe a week and a half. He was stuck in some hotel in Turin in a room with a huge canopied bed.

There was a beep signaling the end of his message and then a long enough pause that I thought the machine had gone into some kind of trance. I could hear breathing, shallow and fast.

"Señorita," the voice whispered. *"Es . . . es Manuela. ¡Ayúdame, por favor! Yo sé que usted me va a ayudar. Veinte uno Westland. ¡Pronto, señorita!"*

I replayed the message because the voice was so soft. It came in gasps and starts, and that made it harder to understand. The Spanish was basic enough: "It's Manuela. Help me, please. I know you will help me. Twenty-one Westland. Hurry."

I tugged at a strand of my hair, a rotten habit that will one day leave me bald. A single hair came loose. I ran it through my fingers.

I've gotten messages like that before, and one thing I have learned is that hurrying to the rescue is one thing and racing off without thinking is another.

I knew where Westland Avenue was, in a student-infested area near Northeastern and the Fens. I thought the voice was Manuela's, but I couldn't be sure. I'm good with voices, but the woman who'd called sounded terrified. Her whispery voice was high and breathy, and I couldn't be sure it belonged to the same woman I'd talked to last night.

Wednesday evening. And it was well into Friday morning now.

Nor did I know when the call had come in.

I'd have to roust Roz, no matter what she and Lemon were up to. I knew Lemon was still around because I'd noticed his van blocking the RESIDENT PARKING ONLY sign. I made my tread especially heavy on the narrow wooden steps leading to the third floor, knocked loudly, and opened the door carefully, which was just as well, because Lemon, clad only in Jockey shorts, was standing behind the door ready to clobber me.

Roz was sound asleep, mouth open, snoring faintly. I roused her by tugging and hollering.

"When did the phone ring?" I asked when she finally sat up, covering herself with the sheet. She sleeps on these tumbling mats she's got all over the floor. Tumbling mats and old black-and-white TVs are her major furniture. It was nice to know she used sheets and pillows. Maybe she'd hauled them out in Lemon's honor.

"Phone," she mumbled.

"There was a call at ten and another maybe half an hour later," Lemon said briskly. I shouldn't have bothered waking Roz.

"Want to earn a few bucks?" I asked Lemon. His illustrious family had cut him off without a cent, and his performance-art career is mainly doing juggling and mime in Harvard Square and passing the hat afterward. I don't know whether Roz pays for her karate lessons or not.

"Sure," he said.

"Me too," Roz said, struggling naked out of the sheets and pulling a selection from her incredible wardrobe of T-shirts over her head. This one was electric blue and said CAPTAIN CONDOM across the front. It was illustrated.

Before we left for Westland Avenue, I dialed Homicide. Mooney wasn't in.

47

8

We took Lemon's van. He drove, and I watched for followers. A cold drizzle slicked the pavements and I huddled in
my peacoat, glad of the warmth of the three of us jammed
in the front seat. Roz sat between us, by virtue of her
barely five foot height, her short legs straddling the hump.
I wasn't sure she was awake at first, but gradually she
came around. I could tell because she started firing questions.

"It's probably nothing," I said.

"Yeah," she replied warily.

"Could be genuine, could be a trap," I said.

"Meet me at the abandoned warehouse at midnight,"
she mumbled. "Expecting anybody in particular?"

"I met an INS agent who doesn't like me," I said. "But
I don't think this is his style."

"Immigration and Naturalization," Lemon said
proudly. He's a bright kid, really.

"If they wanted to know if I knew where the woman
was, they might have faked a help message, but they
wouldn't have given me an address," I said. "They'd have
waited outside the front door to tail me."

"So then it's not the INS," Lemon said. "Probably."

"Yeah. So what I want here is backup. I don't go scooting off in the middle of the night to rescue damsels in distress. Not solo. Not since I read my first Nancy Drew."

"What kind of backup?" Lemon asked.

"I go in alone. I don't come out or give you an all-clear signal in five minutes, you come in."

"You armed?" Roz said, proving she was still awake.

I nodded. My .38 Police Special was tucked in the waistband of my slacks, under my sweater, the metal cold against the small of my back. I keep it in the locked bottom drawer of my desk, unloaded and wrapped in one of my ex-husband's undershirts.

"Okay, then," she said, and seemed to go back to sleep. I didn't have to tell her how much I'd hate to use it. Guns are necessary in the business, what with all the crooks waving them around. I admit that—and I keep my hand in at the pistol range—but I don't like guns. I've killed two men with guns, one when I was a cop, one after I turned private. Both killings had to happen, and I don't spend a lot of time rehashing my life, but neither was easy to swallow.

Lemon drove well, effortlessly shifting the gears on the old van. The rain was the kind of stuff that messes up your windshield, too light for the regular swipe of the windshield blades. The glass steamed up, and Roz leaned forward and wiped a ragged circle with a wad of Kleenex. It fogged again immediately, so we cracked the windows open and froze.

The journey took maybe twenty minutes. Memorial Drive, then over the B.U. Bridge, along Park Drive to Brookline Ave. Lemon took a wrong turn and I had to straighten him out.

The detour took us back along the Fenway, and that's when I noticed the flashing lights. Automobile accident, I told myself, although the first worry pangs hit my stomach just about then. I remembered the newspaper article Manuela had shown me, about the body in the Fens. It must have been found nearby.

Up close I could tell the flashers belonged to police units. No wreckers, no tow trucks. When I saw Mooney's battered Buick parked with two wheels up on the curb, I hollered Lemon to a halt. Then I was out of the car and running, and Lemon was yelling after me, something about where the hell was he supposed to leave the damned van.

I didn't care.

The cops hadn't set up a cordon yet. They were milling and talking, and only one of them tried to head me off, worried I might be the advance press guard. I brushed him off with Mooney's name, and one of the other guys knew me and gave the first guy a wink.

I don't know what Department gossip says about Mooney and me, but it's a hell of a lot more colorful than reality. I'm not a cop now, so it doesn't matter. And yet I guess I still resent it. Otherwise I wouldn't get so pissed, right? Over a simple leering wink from a guy whose IQ was probably a tenth of his badge number.

The old anger gave me something to concentrate on while I sped down the path toward a stand of elms, eerily lit by flashlights and rotating cherry beacons.

Mooney loomed up out of the dark, all six-four two hundred and forty linebacker pounds of him.

"A body?" I said, dreading the answer.

"What are you—"

"Let me see her," I said. "I think I can make the ID."

"It's not pretty," he said.

"It never is."

"Why are you—"

"I got a call. I tried to get you—"

51

"This way," he said. "If you puke, the medical examiner's gonna give me hell."

I followed him, biting my lower lip, hardening myself, getting ready. "Just another stiff," I murmured to myself. "Just another body. Nothing you can do about it. Nothing you can do."

They hadn't bagged it yet. A police photographer stood at her feet and the sudden explosion of light temporarily blinded me.

The height and weight seemed right. The dark hair. The face was bruised and swollen, unrecognizable, cut and covered with dark blood. And the hands were gone. Just gone, hacked off at the wrists.

"Well?" Mooney said.

I couldn't say anything.

Not until I saw something sparkle on the ground.

It was a thin silver band. The filigree ring I'd last seen on my client's left hand.

"Twenty-one Westland Avenue."

I guess I must have mumbled the address as I stared at the dead woman's mutilated arms, because that's what Mooney said to me when he forcibly turned me around by the shoulders.

"Twenty-one Westland," I echoed slowly, looking into his eyes and still seeing the corpse. "Come with me."

"What the hell, Carlotta—"

I started talking and yanking him by the hand at the same time, because I didn't want to lose minutes while I explained. He hollered something over his shoulder to another cop and came with me. I babbled out the tale of the late-night phone call.

"Then you can identify the corpse as the woman who came to see you?"

"The ring on the ground," I said. "She was wearing it."

"Could have been planted," he said.

"It was loose. She kept twisting it, fiddling with it." I remembered her hands—small, hardworking hands with bitten nails.

Lemon had pulled his van onto the grassy verge, shielded by two patrol cars. A cop was quizzing him, and I waved and yelled at him to go on home before he and Roz got arrested.

53

Mooney had two uniforms tail us in a unit. We took his Buick, with me automatically scrambling into the driver's seat and sliding over to the passenger side. Mooney refuses to get his passenger door fixed. He says every time he gets his car shipshape, somebody else bangs into it.

It took us maybe four minutes to find 21 Westland. It shouldn't have taken that long, but none of the apartment buildings, a string of four-story, yellow-brick jobs, seemed to have an address, the same way Boston streets never have street signs. The cross streets sometimes do, but the main thoroughfares, never. It's a way of telling tourists they don't belong.

We finally caught a glimpse of a 43 on a fanlight and got a fix on the proper side of the street. Then we nailed a 57 and turned back, closer to the Fens.

Number 21 didn't seem to have any identifying marks, but it sat next to 23, and that was good enough for me.

There were no parking places. By no parking places I mean *no* parking places. Even the fire hydrants and the handicapped slots were taken. Mooney left the car double-parked with the unit tucked in behind us, its cherry lights flashing. We were both careful to lock our doors, police vehicles not being off-limits to the Massachusetts car thief.

Number 21 was a weathered brick building like the rest, narrow enough to appear taller than its four stories. It had a street lamp close by; from four feet away I could barely make out faint numerals on the cracked glass of the front door.

The door opened easily to a small, dimly lit vestibule; the four of us entering at once made it even smaller. One of the officers in the unit must have been a cigar smoker. I hacked out a cough while we studied our surroundings. There were five mailboxes and five doorbells, which made it one resident per floor and some poor soul in the basement. None of the names under the mailboxes belonged to Manuela Estefan. Nobody had the initials M. E. Mr. Y. Thompson had the top floor, Mr. and Mrs. Keith Moore (Shellie) the third, Lawrence Barnaby the second, R. Freedman the ground floor. The basement apartment was rented out to A. Gaitan, and that was the button Mooney pushed.

I'm not sure if he pushed it because he thought the super might live in the basement or because A. Gaitan had a Hispanic surname.

No response. The cigar-smoking cop was for pushing every goddamn bell until somebody got the hell out of bed and let us the fuck in.

I pressed my nose against the glass of the inside door, and that's when I noticed that someone had slipped a little piece of wood, like half a shim shingle, between the jamb and the door. Nobody was going to have to buzz us in.

There was an elevator in a hallway lit by a single forty-watt bulb. The linoleum on the floor looked like it couldn't stand brighter lighting. There were two doors down the hall past the elevator. One said 1A, so I supposed it belonged to R. Freedman, although I didn't understand the need for the *A* since there was only one apartment per floor. The other door led to a staircase, again lit with a single bare bulb. I glanced at Mooney, and we both nodded at the same time and started down the stairs. One officer followed us. The cigar smoker stayed in the hall, his .38 already out of its unsnapped holster.

The stairway led to a damp corridor lined with old pipes. Somewhere a furnace banged and whimpered. Mooney listened for a moment at the Gaitan apartment

door, then knocked loudly and scooted to one side. The
other officer, taking the cue, flattened himself against a
wall and drew his weapon. I stayed out of the line of fire,
well back in the hallway. I make it a policy never to get in
between guys waving loaded guns.

Nobody answered.

Mooney glared at me. I elevated my shoulders. I
didn't know which apartment the call had come from, any
more than he did. Maybe while we were down here the
killer was escaping out some back door or scrambling
down the fire escape from the fourth-floor apartment.

I was going to urge Mooney to call for more backup
when he got a stubborn set to his jaw, reached over, and
turned the doorknob. It clicked the way doors do when
they're left open, and the eyes of the patrolman who'd
been up against the wall went cold and wary. He shifted
his hands on his gun.

The two cops went through in an instant, noiselessly.
I knew they were checking the rooms, the closets, behind
the doors. That's what cops do first, search for victims and
perps. I went in. Nobody told me not to.

There was no one inside Gaitan's apartment. I could
tell by the deflated air of the young advance cop, his
weapon now sheathed, his adrenaline still pumping.

"Only the two rooms," he muttered, his face pale. He
seemed to be taking extraordinary care with his breathing, in and out, making sure he got it right. "You better see
the other one."

The last comment was addressed to Mooney, but I
tagged along.

The front room was ugly enough, mottled paint, a
sprung beige sofa, two narrow cots, and one wall contain-
ing something an optimistic landlord might describe as a

kitchenette if a two-by-four refrigerator, a hot plate, and a cupboard qualified as a kitchenette.

The back room was worse, much worse. Someone had painted it dull green thirty years ago. A wooden cross bearing an elongated, suffering Jesus was tacked to the back wall. There was barely space for three more narrow cots and a metal rod on wheels that made do for a closet. Two white shirts and two pairs of tan chinos hung crookedly on the rod. The odor of unwashed bedclothes filled the air. That, and something else.

One look, one smell, and Mooney sent the uniform out to fetch a warrant and notify a crime-lab unit. One unmade cot was blood-soaked, rusty in the dim light. Blood had splashed the other two cots, the wall, the cross. An old black dial phone rested on a rumpled pillow, its receiver dangling.

"Don't touch anything," Mooney said sharply.

I gave him a faintly disgusted look. My hands were already in my pockets. They'd made the journey automatically.

"If she'd lost her hands here, the ring might be a plant," I said, just to be saying something. The words came out funny.

"Don't get your hopes up," Mooney said. "Especially if you recognized the voice on the phone . . ."

"I think so, I'm not sure."

"You didn't erase the tape?"

"No."

"Good."

"Think there's enough blood for him to have sawed her hands off here?" I asked.

"How the hell would I know? Depends on whether she was dead or not, how much she'd bleed, I guess."

All the time we were talking, we were looking, the

way cops look at crime scenes, mentally tagging the evidence, asking the questions they'll ask the medical examiner, wondering about fingerprints on the phone, hairs on the pillowcase.

I shivered. "She must have been alone when she called," I said.

"Or somebody might have been holding a knife to her throat," Mooney muttered. Then he seemed to see me for the first time. "You shouldn't be here when the squad arrives," he said.

"I'm a witness," I said.

"To a phone call," he said. "That's all. And maybe you shouldn't get any more involved."

"Involved," I repeated. "She called me for help."

"Look, the INS guy told me this business has nothing to do with stuff here. It's leftovers from Central America. Hit squads. Death squads."

"Mooney," I protested, "I wouldn't believe anything that guy said."

"I don't know what the hell we've got by the tail here," he said sharply, "but I know I don't like it. And I don't like you in the middle of it."

"And there's nothing you can do about it, Mooney," I said evenly, "because here I am. And if I were you, I'd be a hell of a lot more interested in the whereabouts of A. Gaitan than any Salvadoran hit squad."

Mooney opened his mouth to argue. He can't help it. He's Boston Irish, born and bred, and instinct tells him to get the women and children to shelter. He opened his mouth, glared at me, and silently closed his mouth again. Bless him for that.

10

I couldn't sleep when I got home. Big surprise. Roz and Lemon had given up on me and retired for the night, or so the blackness of the third-floor windows seemed to indicate.

No further messages on the machine. I rewound the tape and listened to Manuela's plea, trying to match tone and timbre to the voice I'd heard in my office. I played it again. And again. When I caught myself nodding off, I removed the cassette and slipped it into my handbag.

Upstairs I got ready for bed, splashing noisily in the bathroom sink, humming to crack the silence, undressing and donning one of the men's V-necked T-shirts I prefer as nightwear because they're cheap and comfy with no lacy things that itch. I put on my red chenille bathrobe to ward off a chill that was mainly interior, sat cross-legged on the floor, and yanked the hardshell guitar case out from under the bed.

I used to worry about insomnia, but nobody ever died from it that I know. The best cure I've come up with is my old National steel guitar.

> Me and the devil, we're walking hand in hand.
> Me and the devil, we're walking hand in hand.

I couldn't remember who wrote it, but I was trying to play it the way Rory Block does, with a thumping bass line, making the guitar moan and talk. I can't match Block's voice. She's got too wide a range for me, able to make those low-down groans and then hit those high, wailing shouts. But if I keep in practice, which I try to do, I can damn near imitate her playing. I even bought her instructional tape, because some of her weird tunings and hammerings had me totally frustrated, and I work at it hard.

I have perfect pitch. That and a dollar fifty will get you coffee and a doughnut.

> Bury my body down by the highway sign.
> Bury my body down by the highway sign.

No cheerful stuff tonight.

Usually my eyelids give out before my fingers, but I didn't even try sleep until long after my calluses started to ache. By the time I stretched out on the bed it was almost dawn, and visions of that bloody bed kept yanking me back from the edge of unconsciousness. The alarm clock buzzed way before I was ready for it.

I'd set the alarm for Friday morning volleyball, forgetting that the tournament schedule had effectively canceled it. By the time I quit functioning on automatic pilot, I was at the Central Square Y, feeling fuzzy and disoriented. There weren't enough players for a pickup game, so I ran the track and tacked an extra twenty pool laps to my regular twenty. The pictures in my mind were still ugly. I kept seeing the crucifix on the wall over the stained cot, wondering if it was the last thing Manuela had seen, wondering if it had been any comfort to her.

I dressed and went across the street to Dunkin' Donuts, weaving to avoid the Mass. Ave. traffic, ordered coffee and two honey-dipped as usual, sat at the orange

Formica counter, and reviewed Mooney's moves of the night before.

Letter-perfect. Except for letting me stick around.

He'd talked to every tenant in the building. He'd rousted the owner out of bed as soon as he found out where the rent checks were sent. There was no superintendent in the building. Three buildings, all owned by the same company, shared a super who lived in the basement at 23 Westland. Mr. Perez had been summoned and questioned. He'd rented the basement flat five months ago to a woman named Aurelia Gaitan. She'd paid two months in advance, two months' deposit, and that was the last he'd seen of her. Must have sent in her rent checks or he'd have heard about that, all right. Mr. Canfield, the landlord, didn't put up with any deadbeats, no way, no how. Hispanic lady, yeah. Short, dark. That was all he recalled. Legal, illegal, he didn't know and he didn't care. People had to live someplace, and thank God he'd had somewhere to live before he'd finally gotten his green card, and he was going to be a citizen in maybe three years, and then the police wouldn't wake him in the middle of the night, no, by the Holy Mother, they wouldn't. He'd have some rights then.

And no, he didn't have any idea that more than one woman might have lived in the basement. All these cots, somebody must have moved them in at night while he was sleeping. He had to sleep sometime, didn't he? It was a free country, wasn't it?

He was a short, swarthy, barrel-chested man with a lot of bravado and a bald head. I could tell some of the cops liked Perez as a suspect on the spot. He had an accent and he smelled of liquor and tobacco. But Mooney hadn't been able to shake him, and there was no way to say if he was lying or telling the truth about the woman

61

named Aurelia Gaitan, whether she was my Manuela or not. They had the green card sent over from headquarters, but the super just shrugged when he saw it, saying he sure couldn't tell from a photo the size of a postage stamp whether the two women were the same and what the hell was all the fuss, anyway, and maybe if he were a citizen, he'd call a lawyer or something.

The landlord, Harold Canfield, showed up in a chocolate Mercedes with a lawyer in tow. Aside from the fancy car and the legal help, he didn't fit my image of a landlord. Tall and skinny, with darting eyes and too-short sleeves on his brown suit, he looked like a man who never ate a decent meal. Too much nervous energy for that; he'd just grab a bite standing at the counter the way I sometimes do.

His voice was surprisingly deep and calm. He used it to say that he hadn't a clue as to who was leasing his apartments. All he cared about was getting the rent on time. It was odd, maybe, that the Gaitan woman sent cash in an envelope instead of a check like most of the other tenants, but cash was still legal, wasn't it? And you know how some of these foreigners are, don't hold with banks.

None of the tenants except Lawrence Barnaby admitted seeing anybody associated with the basement flat, and he only said he saw a "Spanish girl" in the hall occasionally. He hadn't even exchanged hellos with her. Maybe he'd seen more than one woman, he wasn't sure. He hadn't paid much attention. Nobody knew anything about the basement flat. Nobody had any idea how many people lived there. Urban isolation.

The index fingerprint on Manuela's green card ought to be some help. The crime lab might be able to tell if she'd been in the apartment.

Of course, there was no finger to match the print to.

I shuddered and spilled a little coffee, wiped it up with a paper napkin.

Scrubbing at the stupid counter top, I realized I wasn't shuddering at the handlessness of the corpse. I've seen worse things than that. You don't stay a cop for six years in Boston without viewing some sights you'd rather not see. What was giving me the shakes was the suspicion, deeply buried in my mind, that I'd pointed the killer at Manuela.

I kept remembering that car, the white Dodge Aries, following me. I'd been so sure it was an INS car, I hadn't even tried to get the plate number. And I'd been so open in my questioning, talking to lawyers, asking for Manuela at the sanctuary church, at the Cambridge Legal Collective.

What if somebody at one of those places had known Manuela, realized I was on her trail, and eliminated her before I could find her? Poor Manuela. Or Aurelia. Or whatever her name really was. The dead woman. The corpse. *La mujer muerta.*

Or worse, what if I'd been home when the phone rang? *I know you will help me.*

I swallowed my last doughnut without tasting it and headed for the car.

11

The Cambridge Episcopal Church of the Transfiguration, the one that offered sanctuary to illegal aliens, was a whitewashed clapboard cube with a steeple set back twenty feet from Massachusetts Avenue. I had more difficulty parking than getting to talk to somebody in authority. Yesterday I'd been treated with suspicion. Today the handful of people busily stuffing envelopes with church newsletters reacted as if I were a leper. They'd evidently read their morning papers.

While I waited, I studied the walls. A poster advertised a Walk for World Peace beginning on Boston Common. Another begged for volunteers to solicit funds by phone. Three quarters of the signs were in Spanish. I picked up a copy of a handout newspaper, the *Central American Reporter*, the monthly outlet of CASA, the Central America Solidarity Association. BETWEEN WOMEN THERE ARE NO BOUNDARIES was the headline on the front page. I read an article on a women's peace convoy to Central America. One of the women in the convoy had met with Pancho Villa's granddaughter.

"Follow me, please," a cold voice said. "Father Emmons will see you."

I was ushered into his office by one of the starch-faced women who'd given me the brush-off yesterday. She handed my card to a man seated at an oak desk and gave me a withering look. I assumed it was meant to reek of pity or piety, but I wasn't sure which.

The minister pushed aside a stack of papers he appeared to be sorting into three unequal piles, stared at my card for a while, and, by means of a curt nod, invited me to sit across from his desk in a straight-backed chair. He was a stoop-shouldered man of over fifty with graying hair, graying skin, and a thin, sharp nose. His eyes were pale watery blue. They reflected the gray of his suit and fit into the overall monochrome. A pot of red geraniums on the corner of the desk seemed positively flamboyant.

"So you're the one," he said very quietly, almost as if he were conducting a conversation with himself.

I intruded. "The one what?" I asked.

"They gossip." He made a vague gesture that included everyone from his immediate staff to the world in general. He didn't seem to know where to put my card, whether to return it to me or to file it in one of the piles on his desk. "I tell them that gossip can hurt the people we work with, harm them beyond measure, but they gossip nonetheless, and your visit here was, uh, a topic of conversation even before they read about the poor woman's death, about which I'm somewhat confused, since she seems to have died twice in the newspapers."

"They misidentified an earlier corpse," I said tersely, not wanting to explain further, although his watery eyes invited confidences. The rest of his face was curiously immobile; only the eyes seemed really alive.

He made a rumble deep in his throat, coughed into a white handkerchief, and continued his conversation with himself. "They do gossip, I'm afraid. This has made quite a sensation. And now, of course . . ." His voice faded.

"What?" I asked. "Do they have me pegged as the leader of some right-wing hit squad? Reverend, I assure you—"

"You have no reason to assure me of anything," he said gently. "I'm not accusing you." He glanced up at me suddenly, and his eyes no longer seemed vague. "Why did you come here?"

"You'd make a good cop," I said admiringly. "Catch a lot of people off guard."

"The question remains," he said, flushing a little and moving paper from one pile to another, shielding his embarrassment at having been caught in the eye trick.

"Do you trust the people who work for you?" I asked bluntly.

He raised his eyes again, and they were mild this time, under control. "What do you mean, 'trust'?"

"I mean, how do you get to work here, in this program to save refugees?"

"You walk in the front door and volunteer," he said.

"I see," I said. "It's very selective."

"It is," he agreed. "Hard work. You'd be surprised how that narrows the numbers."

"How can you be sure you're not employing somebody who also works for, say, a right-wing death squad?"

"How can I be sure you're not going to pull a gun on me this minute?" he responded.

"You can't," I said.

He shuffled a few more papers. "One takes a lot on trust."

I waited until he looked at me again, then asked, "Are you a trusting man?"

His lips almost formed a smile. "I trust that my fellow humans have all their share of foibles and maybe a few extra kinks I haven't seen before. I'm a priest, but I live in the world."

"Do any of your volunteers seem odd?"

"All my volunteers provoke gossip, about the way they dress and the way they raise their children, but none is a suspected spy, if that's the meaning of your question."

"That's the meaning of my question."

He shuffled papers for a time. I let the silence grow. "Any other questions?" he said finally.

"Yes. Did anyone besides me ever ask about Manuela Estefan?"

"I've communicated all I know to the police."

"About me?" I asked.

"Yes. The women you talked to yesterday gave a fairly accurate description. The red hair, you know. And the height."

"Did they describe anybody else?"

"No," he said.

"Did you know Manuela?"

"Me? No, but I don't make contact with every one of our refugees."

"Was she known here?" I said, thinking the man would make a good crook as well as a good cop. He answered only what you asked him, didn't volunteer information.

"No," he said. "She was not known here. Not until you asked for her."

"I'm here because I want—I need—to make sure her death isn't connected to my coming here."

"I see," he said. "You feel guilt."

Ah, yes, I thought. That's it. Good old guilt. I considered telling this holy minister of God a little about my childhood, about being raised in a half Jewish, half Catholic home by a union-organizing bleeding-heart mother. "It's all right to beat yourself for your sins," she used to say in Yiddish, "but don't enjoy the punishment too much."

"Guilt is my middle name," I said instead.

"It does no good."

"I know, I know," I said. "It won't bring back the dead, right?"

He took a deep breath, and his face got almost animated. "I mean that I counsel against guilt in general, but not entirely. I believe in owning up to one's sins. If you feel that you sinned against Manuela by asking about her here, I hope you're wrong. We seek to help these people, not harm them."

"Me too," I said. "But you can never be sure, can you?"

He bowed his head.

"But you do what you can," I said.

He looked up and his eyes were clear. "I believe in taking action," he said, "if one believes one is morally justified."

"Me too," I said, holding his glance.

"I haven't answered any of your questions," he said.

"Yes, you have," I said.

The volunteer women buzzed like angry bees as I left his office and walked down the aisle between the pews toward the door.

Outside, I found a pay phone. One of the lawyers I'd spoken to yesterday was out of town, the other one swore he hadn't mentioned my queries to anyone and wanted to know everything I knew about the murder. I told him to read it in the *Herald*.

12

My next stop was up Mass. Ave. and into North Cambridge, at the Cambridge Legal Collective, a storefront operation that probably spent more on rent than they did on upkeep or impressing the neighbors. Their logo was hand lettered on a square of cardboard and masking-taped to the door. Another sign read: PLEASE KNOCK BEFORE ENTERING and *por favor toque antes de entrar.* So I knocked and went in. The sign didn't say you had to wait.

I was hoping for a different secretary, but the same guy who'd treated me like an INS spy was behind the metal desk, speaking rapid-fire Spanish into a phone. He glared at me. I sat down on a folding chair, one of many lined up against the far wall, and decided he had no need to worry about privacy as long as he kept up the clip. I could only catch a few words, and out of context they didn't mean a thing to me. I was practically in the dark until *"Hasta luego."*

"You again," he said as soon as he got off the phone.

"Nice to see you too," I said. He blushed, being one of those fair-haired guys who do that, and I felt I'd scored a hit, however minor. I bit my lip. This was a guy whose cooperation I needed.

A woman came out of the back room wearing a navy-blue pin-striped suit and a pale blue bow-collared silk blouse that probably cost more than my entire closetful of Filene's Basement cast-offs. Her bag and shoes were gray with navy piping, her glasses looked like props she kept around to make people take her seriously. Harvard Law, class of '87, I thought. Maybe '88.

I was on my feet before she'd taken two steps. I cut her off at the door.

"Carlotta Carlyle," I said, holding out my hand and betting she was too well bred not to take it.

She had a firm, cool grip.

"I'm a detective," I said while the guy at the desk tried to start a sentence several times and failed.

"We need to talk," I said. "About one of your clients."

"I already told the other officer everything."

Bingo, I said to myself.

Harvard Law glanced at her expensive wristwatch and sighed. "Come in the back, please," she said. "I really do want to cooperate, but I wish you'd coordinate things better so I didn't have to plow the same ground over and over again."

This from a woman who probably specialized in taking depositions.

I kept the smirk of triumph off my face as we bypassed the secretary and headed for the inner office.

Miss Harvard sat behind a desk with another eloquent sigh and gestured me into one of the card-table rejects in front of it. I sat, my tailbone protesting the icy metal. The Cambridge Legal Collective didn't spend a lot on heat either. I kept my windbreaker on. What I don't get at Filene's Basement I buy at the Army-Navy Surplus Store in Central Square. Miss Harvard probably shopped at Bonwit Teller. Maybe eight hundred bucks for the suit.

"So," she said. Trust a lawyer to give a lot away.

"Manuela Estefan. Did you help her get her green card?"

"Is that the woman the other officer asked about?" She wasn't being nasty, just trying to remember. "No, I did not get her the green card. And neither did anybody else associated with the Collective."

"But you recognized the name."

"Because of the newspapers," she said. "And that policeman. I wish he'd caught one of the other counselors." Her look said plainly that she wished I had too.

Damn.

"You're a lawyer," I said, plainly fishing.

"I'm sorry," she responded like the lady she was. "Marian Rutledge. I work for Blaine and Foreman, but I volunteer here—along with a lot of others."

Blaine and Foreman was a big-time downtown firm. That accounted for the clothes.

"So Manuela had no connections here? No friends?"

"She may have had friends among the other immigrants, but I wouldn't know about that. I checked our files and she didn't come in to see us. We weren't contacted about her by any government agency. Not until after her death."

I wished I knew if the police had been in touch after my Manuela's first supposed, or second actual, demise, but I couldn't risk the question. It was sheer luck that Marian Rutledge had mistaken me for a detective from the Boston Police. I put it down to lack of experience on her part. I didn't want to do anything to make her question her assumption, nor did I wish to do anything to make myself liable to a claim that I'd knowingly impersonated a police officer.

I said, "Sometimes you are contacted by the government?"

"Often," she replied. "Say an immigrant has worked with the Human Rights Commission in El Salvador, well, we have people on our staff who used to work with that commission and who'd be willing to take on the case. So the government sends the immigrant from one of the detention camps—"

I'd stopped thinking of the U.S. in terms of detention camps since they'd rounded up the Japanese during World War II. And that was just something in history books. "Detention camps," I repeated.

"They prefer detention 'centers,'" Marian Rutledge said with a grim smile, "but they look like camps. Overcrowded. Barbed wire. The biggest one is in Harlingen, Texas. They might release an inmate of Harlingen on bond and send him or her up here to have the case heard by a Boston Immigration and Naturalization judge. It's happening less and less. They keep them in Harlingen now. Say it speeds up the hearing process, but that's not necessarily true. The courts are crowded up here, but down there, well, they're logjammed."

She'd stopped glancing at her watch and I got the feeling that this was the part of her work she liked and that Blaine and Foreman and all their pricey civil and property cases could go hang.

"Most of the cases we handle are political refugees. Applications for asylum. And less than one percent of our people ever make the cut."

"That's not a whole hell of a lot," I said, because she seemed to want some response.

"They say the Salvadorans just come here for jobs— and the Nicaraguans too—but if they go back, they'll be shot. Herbert Anaya, the director of the Human Rights Commission, was shot to death," she continued indignantly, "right outside his own home. These aren't frivolous cases. These are life-and-death cases."

"So it's hard for a Central American to get a green card."

"Damn near impossible," Marian Rutledge said.

"Tell me, are there rumors about Salvadoran death squads around here?"

"If there are, I haven't heard any," she said. "I've heard rumors about groups operating in Miami and L.A. And Texas. Those are the major ports of call. Boston is pretty small potatoes for immigrants from Central America. Too cold. We get a lot of Irish, but they aren't treated half so badly."

"And what about counterfeiting?"

"Counterfeiting?" she said.

"Documents," I countered.

"You mean, working papers, Social Security cards? It's getting worse since the Immigration Act of '86, but I don't know what else the government expected. If staying home means dying, a lot of people are going to come up here, documents or no documents. And if you have to show documents to work, even with a labor shortage, well, I'm not siding with the counterfeiters, but I probably wouldn't turn one in to the INS either."

I like lawyers who aren't too stuck on the law. I smiled at her, and she seemed quite human in spite of her clothes.

"Any green-card counterfeiting?" I asked.

She shook her head. Her long brown hair swung from side to side.

"It's too fancy a job," she said. "I haven't heard of any counterfeit green cards. But if anybody did figure out how to get a good one, well, that would open the way for all the other documents. Once you've got a green card, you're practically a citizen. Home free."

"Right," I said.

She glanced at her watch again, and this time she stood up. "I've got to go," she said, sticking out her hand. "Nice meeting you, and I'm relieved you didn't want me to look at any more of those awful pictures. All those poor women."

All those poor women.

"Just a minute," I said. "What pictures are you talking about?" I'd already decided the police must have questioned her right after the first victim had been identified. There hadn't been enough time since my Manuela's death. Surely she would have commented if I'd been the second cop of the day. So what "poor women," in the plural, was she talking about?

"Is this a case of the right hand not knowing what the left is doing or what?" she asked.

I thought we'd built up some sort of rapport and decided now was as good a time as any to test it. I pulled out one of my business cards, which do not feature the Boston Police shield.

"Private," she snorted, if anyone that classy could be said to snort, "and I fell for it."

"I won't tell anybody," I said. "Please. I know I've used up plenty of your time, but I need to know about those photographs."

"Why? What business is it of yours? Who are you working for?"

"A dead woman," I said.

She sat back down and sucked in a deep breath. "What do you want to know about the photos?" she asked. "They were just a lot of gruesome scene-of-the-crime shots. I don't want to look at any more of them."

"One scene or two?"

"Two," she said. "Maybe three."

"And this was when?" I asked, swallowing. "This morning?"

"Two days ago."

The image came back to me so strongly, I could have drawn a picture of it: Mooney's door with pushpins on a map. Three of them.

13

That map was the first thing I looked at when I stormed into Mooney's office thirty minutes later. I banged the door shut, and there it was, with an added pushpin. Number four. Representing the second Manuela Estefan. *My* Manuela Estefan.

"Why the hell didn't you tell me?" I demanded, not giving Mooney a chance to say hello or what's up or get out. "Why isn't it in the papers? Because they're poor women? Because they're illegals, Hispanics, nobodies? Somebody kills off a bunch of rich white Brahmin ladies, I bet it makes the morning news."

The corners of Mooney's mouth tightened. "We've caught—what—seventy-eight homicides so far this year," he said flatly. "Some of them hardly rate a paragraph. You know that."

"Maybe if I'd known that other killing was part of a string, I would have looked harder for Manuela."

"You think we weren't looking for her? You think there wasn't an APB?"

"But if—"

"If," Mooney interrupted, his voice harsh. "Didn't you grow out of 'if' when you were a cop?"

I sank into the wooden chair on the far side of his desk. There was a long silence, punctuated by breathing

79

and the distant sound of ringing phones. I finally broke it. "Sorry, Mooney," I said. "Driving here in the car, I got so mad, I had to blow up at somebody."

He nodded and I took that to mean we were still on speaking terms.

I jerked my head back to indicate the map on his door. "Four dead."

"I hope you didn't read it in the *Herald.*"

"No."

"Four months, four corpses. We didn't get a lot from the first one. It was badly decomposed by the time we found it, so it may be just three—"

"Three's enough," I said.

"Plenty," Mooney agreed, "but there could be more. Now that we're pretty sure we're dealing with a serial, we put out the alarm. Calls will start to come in. The bodies we've got were all found in urban parks, the Emerald Necklace chain, but every hick-town officer who finds a dog bone will get in touch."

"M.O.?"

"Strangles them, then uses a knife to carve them up."

"Molested?"

"Can't be sure on most of them. This last one, no. We got to the body soon enough to tell."

"How soon?" It was a question I wasn't sure I wanted to ask.

"Three hours, maybe."

That fit with the time of Manuela's call. Again I wondered what would have happened if I'd been home to answer the damn phone. I dug into my bag and handed Mooney the cassette with Manuela's call, wishing Sam's voice weren't on it as well. Mooney knows about Sam. He doesn't approve.

"How'd you find the body?" I asked.

"Dumb luck. Late-night jogger spotted it. He's clean."
Mooney's hand swallowed the cassette and he carefully
placed it in one of the few rectangles where his desktop
showed through. "Thanks. I don't know how it's gonna
help, but thanks."

"You want me to try the ID again?" I asked reluctantly. "Maybe with her face cleaned up . . . ?"

"The M.E. did his best. Got somebody in from a fu-
neral home. We got a video you could look at."

"Here? Pretty high-tech." I was relieved. The smell at
Southern Mortuary is not something I relish.

"Interrogation Room Two," Mooney said. "We moved
a set in there. It's some federal-funds stunt, but I like it.
We don't have to keep sending guys over to Southern." He
pushed back his chair. "Well, wanna get it over with?"

"Sure." I followed him out the door.

Mooney turned out the lights in the windowless interrogation room. The TV square seemed to float in dark-
ness. I waited, trying not to think about Manuela, while
Mooney pressed buttons and cursed. The screen suddenly
showed her face, the dark hair fanned out against a stark
white cloth. Cleaned up, most of the cuts seemed superfi-
cial. One cheek had been sutured together. Her skin was
mottled.

"Yeah," I said.

On the way out of the room I realized I'd been holding my breath, trying not to smell odors that weren't
there.

"Coffee?" Mooney asked.

"Nah."

When we were seated on opposite sides of his desk
again, I said, "It's too clean. I'd almost rather go to the
morgue. The morgue's real. This feels like some TV show,
like it didn't really happen, only I know it did."

81

"Next round of budget cuts, we'll probably have to sell the videocam," Mooney said. "That ought to make you happy."

"Delirious," I said unenthusiastically.

"So how'd you dope it out?" Mooney asked after a long pause. "The serial angle. You see the map on the door?"

"Cops showed crime-scene photos to a Cambridge Legal Collective lawyer," I explained. "Too many crime scenes. I take it this is not for publication."

"Think it would do any good?" Mooney asked. "Giving the guy free publicity?"

There's practically nothing I hate more than sensational serial-killer headlines. They're so goddamn misleading. First of all, the overwhelming number of murder victims are male, mostly young black males killed in gang violence or drug disputes or just because they live and work in the wrong place. Do they wind up on page one? No way. But let some weirdo start killing women and it's everywhere, in eighteen-point screamers. And the victims are always described as "attractive" and "young," as if the weirdo were auditioning bathing beauties or something, as if the women had incited the crimes.

Go ahead, show me an account of a male murder victim that uses the word *handsome.*

"Well," I muttered lamely, "women who fit the pattern might be more cautious about who they go out with."

"What's the pattern?" Mooney asked.

"You tell me."

"I'd have liked to ask your Manuela Estefan," he said.

"Me too," I murmured, shaking my head.

"When the papers do get this, we'll be up to our ears," Mooney said, "mostly backlash from the Weld Square stuff. Nobody picked up on that till there were six dead and I don't remember how many missing."

"How come?"

"Bodies found in different areas. Different cops, different medical examiners. Victims connected to prostitution and drugs, not women who led regular nine-to-five lives, not ladies the suburban reader would relate to. And there's stupidity," he added, glaring at the phone on his desk as though he'd already received too much of that commodity over the receiver. "You can't rule that out."

I said, "You called the dead woman, the woman I just saw, *my* Manuela Estefan. Do you think that was her name?"

"Carlotta," he said, reaching across the desk as if he could pat my hand and make it all better.

"Jesus," I said, drawing back. "A simple yes or no will get me off your back."

"Goddamn, what's eating you?" he said. "If I had a simple yes or no, I'd dish it out. But you're asking a tough one. Was your Manuela really Manuela? Well, let me ask you a few of the ones that go with that. Who is Manuela? Who is Aurelia Gaitan?"

I'd forgotten the Gaitan name for a minute, had to remember that it was the name of the basement-apartment tenant with the bloody bed.

"Nobody's seen Aurelia Gaitan since the dead woman was found," Mooney continued.

"Her prints must be in the apartment."

"And what have we got to match them to? The Manuela Estefan green card, right? Well, what's on a green card? One lousy index print. We've sent over to INS for the full set, but even if we got a match, it would only mean that the woman on the green card was in that apartment sometime within the last six months or so."

83

"I'm asking about my Manuela. Could the green card be hers? She doesn't look exactly like the photo, but, hell, I'd hate to think people could identify me from my driver's license shot."

"We couldn't match fingerprints. The killer took care of that. I thought we'd be able to check ears; when you get photographed for your green card, your right ear has to show. But your lady's ears were carved up too. So we brought in a photo expert. He blew up the Estefan shot and matched the features—distance between the eyes and stuff like that. He says your woman was not Estefan. If, of course, that's Manuela Estefan's picture on the green card." Mooney blew out a deep breath. "Four women dead and we don't have a decent ID on one of them. How the hell can people just disappear and nobody cares enough to fill out a form?"

He didn't expect an answer. I said, "Well, do you have anything on the killer?"

He tapped a precarious stack of paper on one corner of his desk. "About a million things that don't add up to shit," he said. *"Número uno,* the guy is smart."

"Guy?"

"You know the stats on serials," he said.

"Why smart?"

"Because he washes up, that's why. He's real neat. Compulsive. There's not a trace of him in that room so far, except maybe some smudged prints on the underside of the toilet seat."

"I want to know about the other women. Is there a connection to—to my Manuela?" I couldn't think about her without a name.

"Goddammit, if there were, I couldn't tell you about it. Carlotta, you aren't a policewoman, right? So you can't get into this, even if the woman was more to you than you say."

"Fishing for something, Mooney?"

"I'm assuming you didn't leave anything out of your story."

"Why?"

"Because you know what withholding evidence can do to a case."

"Is the INS following me?" I asked.

"Do I look like a psychic? Ask them."

"Why is INS involved? Why not the FBI?"

"INS. FBI. Everybody's involved now. It's alphabet soup. You wanna see the paperwork? I got VI-CAP crime sheets coming out of my ears, and most of the stuff they want to know, I got to leave blank because I haven't got the faintest idea." He pulled another stack of papers over in front of him and started reading aloud angrily, his index finger stabbing the page. "The stuff on last days of the victim is where I really shine, because we don't know where the hell any of these women spent any of their days. Think we should maybe put their pictures in the paper, the way they looked dead, so people could identify them? Think the mayor would like that? Then maybe I could do these goddamn profile sheets and send 'em off to Quantico and everybody'd get off my case. Here. You want to fill out the recent-life-experience sheet? Just keep checking the 'unknown' box."

I stood up and went around behind his desk. The familiar set of his shoulders and the nape of his tanned neck looked very dear to me, and I considered rubbing his back, thought about the hard muscle underneath the blue broadcloth.

"I'm sorry," I said. "You haven't slept at all, have you?"

"What's that got to do with it?"

85

"Nothing," I said, and I turned around and walked out. I could hear him calling after me but I didn't stop.

Someday Mooney and I may get our gears in sync, but for years now it's been like this. I get sympathetic, he gets defensive; he gets sympathetic, I boil. Chemistry. It's the damnedest thing.

14

I reclaimed the car. The expired meter said I'd violated the parking laws, but no one had caught me at it. I felt a warm glow at the sight of my ticketless window.

My satisfaction lasted the length of the B.U. Bridge, which I almost always choose over the Longfellow. Longfellow's too crowded. I could have taken the Mass. Ave. Bridge, the one closest to Marta's apartment, but construction's got the traffic so fouled up, I haven't crossed it in years. The Mass. Ave. Bridge, which is really named the Harvard Bridge, is a joke. It's right near M.I.T., but rumor says the Techie engineers didn't want their name sullied by such an architectural botch and gracefully allowed Harvard the honor—and the snickers that accompany it each time the bridge needs to be closed for repairs. Now the state's in the process of rebuilding it completely, and the real confrontation is over whether or not to renew the Smoots.

Smoot was an M.I.T. student in the early sixties or so, and one night his frat brothers got the idea of spray-painting the bridge in Smoot-lengths. Whether they picked him up and carried him along, lying him down and using him as a gigantic ruler, or whether they made him roll over the bridge-marking his shoulder-to-shoulder width as a single "Smoot," is an item of hot debate. It made both local papers, proving the late Andy Warhol right.

Smoots kept my mind clicking most of the way to Marta's, so I didn't start worrying about whether she'd lied to me about knowing Manuela until I started looking for a parking place. Sometimes it seems as if my days are one continual search for a parking place. That's probably why I like driving a cab. You never need a space.

A car pulled out up the street, maybe five hundred yards ahead, and I gunned the Toyota into the slot before somebody could ace me out of it. A sign at the curb read RESIDENT PARKING ONLY. I parked even though I had the wrong color resident sticker. My area of Cambridge has a different color code. Resident parking stickers follow a bizarre color code even most meter maids can't crack. I hoped the one on this beat hadn't figured it out.

The car in front of me was a white one, late-model, boxy. It reminded me of the white Aries.

Either Marta wasn't home or she wasn't answering the damn door. I thought she might be ignoring the bell, what with her arthritis kicking up, so after pounding on the door for fifteen minutes I found an unvandalized pay phone and punched her number. I let the line ring twenty times, then slammed the receiver back into the cradle.

The door to Marta's building opened, and an old man came out, bent and stooped, with a jaunty hat covering his head. His skin was beaded with liver spots, but behind heavy glasses his eyes seemed bright.

"Hi," I said.

He seemed to shrink within himself and hastily clasped the pocket of his worn tan windbreaker. I now knew where he kept his wallet.

"Hello," I said again, quietly.

"What do you want?" I couldn't make out the accent at first. He didn't look Hispanic or anything. He just looked old, a country all its own.

"You Mr. Binkleman?" I asked. There was a Bin-kleman on the mailbox at Marta's. It was the only name I could remember.

"No. There's no Mr. Binkleman, only Mrs. Bin-kleman. On the first floor in the back." His voice pleaded with me to go away. He was walking all the time he spoke, his legs moving fast but his stride so restricted by the lack of swing in his joints that he had no chance of escaping me.

"Look, I'm not going to rob you. I'm a friend of the lady on two with the five kids."

"They make a racket, those kids."

"Have you seen Marta today, the mother?"

"Why?"

"I was supposed to have lunch with her. She must have forgotten," I said.

"Must have," he said. "She went to work this morn-ing."

"Work?"

"You're not from the Welfare, are you?" He stopped trying to walk and risked a glance at my face. I think he was surprised that he had to look up so far.

"No."

"Good. I wouldn't talk to nobody from the Welfare. It's no sin being poor, you know. It's no sin being old. I deserve what I get from Social Security. It's no handout. It's just what I paid in, is all."

I decided not to tell him that what he'd paid in had been inflation-eaten to the point it probably wouldn't have bought a round-trip ticket to Miami Beach. He'd probably worked hard all his life, and he wasn't lounging in any lap of luxury now.

I asked, "How do you know Marta went to work?"

"Her cousin, Lilian or something, picks her up in the

car sometimes and then she goes to work, I think. She's got more money then, anyway. Pizzas get delivered. Rent checks get mailed. You know."

"You're observant," I said.

"Those kids make a lot of noise. I'm not deaf. God's saving that for later, maybe."

"Yeah," I said. "Well, how's your eyesight? Was she using her cane this morning?"

"No. But she looked like she should have been using it. Thank God I don't need a cane yet. It's a pity to see it in a young woman. Thank God old age didn't hit me till I was old."

We'd made it halfway to the dusty playground in the center of the housing project. The old man's breathing was audible, his face redder than when we'd started our walk.

"You need a ride somewhere?" I asked.

"You're from the Welfare, aren't you, and I'm shooting off my mouth. I didn't mean anything I said. I'm old, I run on at the mouth. I live alone. Sometimes I have long conversations with my dog."

"I'm not from Welfare, honest, and I'd be glad to drive you where you need to go."

"Need," he said, making a noise somewhere between a cough and a laugh. "That's a good one. Look, I don't need much these days. And the reason I'm out here putting my feet down is because some kid doctor tells me I need the exercise. I used to like to walk, but I liked to walk at night in the glow from the street lamps, when it's nice and cool. You walk now under the street lamps, you better keep your will in your pocket. So I go out in the daytime, but I don't like it so much. You can see all the dog turds on the street."

"At night you just step on them," I said.

"Yeah," he said, "but I liked it better that way."

"Thanks for the chat," I said. "Nice meeting you."

"We didn't meet," he said, sticking out a bony hand. "I'm Hank Binkleman."

"You said there wasn't any Mr. Binkleman—"

"Yeah, I didn't know what you wanted, right? I don't tell people who I am anymore."

"And is there a Mrs. Binkleman, or did you make that up too?"

"She's dead fifteen years."

"I'm sorry."

"But about your friend I didn't lie. She left early this morning, right after the kids went to school."

"Thanks."

"You're welcome."

He inched on, scuffing up small clouds of playground dust. I walked over to Paolina's school.

One of the few things I like about the Cambridge public schools is that they don't have middle schools or junior high schools or whatever the hell you call them, where they segregate the seventh-, eighth-, and ninth-graders from the rest and put all the truly unmanageable, hormones-out-of-control kids in one building and write it off. Paolina will go to her grade school until it's time to hit Cambridge Rindge and Latin, a building big enough to remind me of my own Detroit high school.

Paolina's school is on Cambridge Street. Her teacher is Mrs. Keegan, a sweet Quaker lady I've met when accompanying Marta to parent-teacher conferences. Marta doesn't like to go alone because of her English and because of her arthritis. She says I make a better impression with the teachers, being American-born, and I hope she's wrong, but Marta's pretty sharp. I like Mrs. Keegan because Mrs. Keegan likes Paolina.

There was a second teacher in the room, a younger woman, maybe a student teacher. She gave me a dour look. In low tones Mrs. Keegan explained that the students were in the middle of their art lesson. I assured her my visit would take no time at all and really was urgent. She called Paolina's name.

I could hear a snort and some laughter and a few quick words of Spanish from a cracking adolescent male voice. Seemed like the visiting art teacher wasn't totally in control.

When Paolina appeared, her cheeks looked hot.

"What did that kid say?" I asked. "I couldn't understand it. You're not teaching me the right slang."

"Nada," she said. "He's a goon. Most of the kids here are real space cadets."

Maybe the red cheeks had nothing to do with the boy's words, the answering giggles. Maybe she was just embarrassed at being singled out. She's shy in class. I keep trying to encourage her to open up and ask more questions, but Marta tells her the opposite, so she's a little confused.

Marta doesn't really believe in school. Not for girls. It makes me grind my teeth at night.

"How are you, sweetie?" Paolina winced and turned to make sure the door was shut.

"Sorry," I amended. "How are you, kiddo?"

She was wearing a checked shirt and a denim blue-jean skirt with a lot of showy gold seam-stitching, the kind that looks like it was made by some trendy designer. Marta made it for her last birthday. Give Marta some fabric and a break from the arthritis and you've got a new outfit.

Paolina said, "You checking to see if I'm in school?"

"I wouldn't have to haul you out of class for that, would I?"

She was twisting a piece of gold wire in her hands.

"What's that?" I asked, stalling for time. She seemed angry and annoyed. I needed a chance to figure out this new moody sister of mine.

She held it out on the palm of her hand. At first I thought it was some kind of fancy paper clip.

"It's like a stick man," I said. "Nice. For a pin?"

She turned it sideways. "It's a fish," she said. "For a pendant."

Batting a thousand, I thought.

"Are you taking me out?" she asked.

"No."

"Too bad."

"Why?"

"I'm bored," she said.

"Let me see the fish." When you looked at it from the right angle, it was an elegant design. Simple. The basic shape depended on only one twist of the fine wire, but Paolina had spiraled the entire span before starting, so the fish seemed more complex than it was.

"I can't go to your game tomorrow," Paolina said.

"I'm sorry. I need my cheering section. But I can pick you up afterward."

"Not afterward, either. I can't see you tomorrow. Probably I'm not supposed to talk to you at all."

"Why?"

"I dunno," she said, staring at the floor tile as if the checkerboard pattern were about to rearrange itself. "Look, I better get back in before Miss Lenox blows her top."

I put my hand on her shoulder. "Sweetie, I need to

find your mother, and I'm not sure where she's working today."

"Don't call me 'sweetie,' okay?"

"Old habits die hard."

"And my mom doesn't work, you know that." Paolina's voice gets higher when she's angry. Two disks of color appeared on her cheeks.

"Paolina, I'm not trying to catch her—"

"I'm not supposed to talk about it. Marta said I'm not."

"Like you're not supposed to know any Manuela Estefan?"

"I don't know her. I don't." Her gaze moved a little higher, maybe to the tops of her shoes.

"Paolina, this business about Manuela Estefan is important. If you know her, if you've ever heard the name—"

"I said I don't know her."

"I don't want to scare you—" I began slowly.

"Then don't," she cut in. "Everybody's always saying tell me this or tell me that. And don't tell this and don't tell that. I can't even keep it straight anymore. I can't—"

Her lower lip wobbled, but she gulped down a deep breath and straightened her shoulders. I haven't seen her cry in maybe a year. She used to cry a lot when she was seven. I wondered when it was she'd quit, and I hoped I didn't have anything to do with her switch to stoicism.

Before I could say another word, she was gone, inside the classroom, slamming the door behind her. I stood in the doorway and watched her take her seat, head held high, blinking back tears.

Talk to me, I wanted to shout. Talk to me.

15

The Huntington Avenue Y is not in the best part of town, but neither is it in the worst. It has plenty of prestigious neighbors, like Symphony Hall, the Mother Church, the New England Conservatory, and Northeastern University, so the area is dense with music lovers, followers of Christian Science, music students, and students in general. I did myself a favor and left the car home. Instead I caught the Dudley bus from Harvard Square. It came within five minutes of my arrival at the stop, miracle of miracles, and I climbed aboard, trailing my gym bag. I didn't nab a seat, but I hadn't expected to.

Kristy, our captain, best setter, and coach, was already dressed and warming up. The others were straggling in. I joined the stragglers in the locker room to change to crotch-cutter shorts, long-sleeved top, knee pads, socks, and sneakers. The locker room boasted cement walls painted a pale green, matching battered lockers, mirrors plenty high enough for midgets, and that comforting high school sweat-sock-and-mold aroma.

I changed quickly and went out to join Kristy. After I stretched my muscles out, we went to work on a spike-and-dig drill. The gym filled slowly. I was concentrating on the drill, but I could tell by the increasing volume.

A whistle sounded. Five minutes to game. My team

95

huddled on the far side of the gym, and Kristy gave us a brief lecture on the perils of overconfidence. Our opponent today was from the western suburbs, and we'd decided long ago that they were the patsies of the finals, a team that would run screaming if their fingernail polish got chipped. An unfair assessment, maybe, but the 'burbs have that reputation in tough old Central Square, Cambridge. Their team was called the Butterflies. Hardly awe-inspiring. We're the Y-Birds, which I always think sounds like jailbirds. Far as I know, we have no ex-cons among us.

Kristy tried to give them a buildup, but the truth of the matter was they were a one-woman team. She was supposed to be quite something and I'd given her more than a passing glance when she came into the gym. She was a Boston College player, banned from their team for flunking grades. A former National Team player, six-four if she was an inch, blond, agile, and aggressive by repute.

Our basic game plan was to keep the ball out of her hands.

The whistle blew; we all slapped hands and ran out onto the court. There was a smattering of applause. I didn't even look over at the bleachers. Paolina wasn't there.

"Who's the hunk?" Samantha, a middle blocker, murmured in my ear. She's some kind of computer programmer. She has count-the-house eyes and rarely misses a setup shot.

I'm an outside hitter. I sent my eyes along the stands in the direction of her nod and found the guy she had to mean, sitting alone three rows behind our team bench. Hunk didn't do him justice.

I shrugged, reached down, and touched the floor with my palms. My back felt a little tight.

The ref tossed the coin and it went our way. Kristy stood in to serve and the ref did a quick check to make sure we were all in position.

The first game went as expected. When someone made the mistake of serving near Miss Boston College, we lost the point. But there were five other players on the court, and while B.C. tried to cover as much ground as possible, the others weren't helping her. There was one small brunette who practically stood there imitating a fireplug. B.C. was starting to steam when we took the first game 15–6.

Between games, Edna informed us that the hunk was an Olympic scout sent to check out B.C., the Olympics having lower academic standards than Boston College. Edna's friend, Joy, maintained the hunk was the fireplug's fiancé, but nobody believed her. Conjure up faces to go with those names: Edna and Joy. Then I'll tell you that Edna, who has a wicked serve, is our team beauty, and Joy is as plain and dour as they come.

"So if he's here to scout B.C., how come he's watching Carlyle's every move?" Kristy asked.

I glanced at her, surprised. And I admit, I gave the hunk another once-over as well.

He had sandy hair, longish but well cut and gleaming clean. Late twenties, early thirties. An athlete's thick neck and wide, sloping shoulders. A broad face, maybe a little chin-heavy. Couldn't tell the color of the eyes, but for some reason I assumed they'd be blue.

We took the second game. This one was tougher because B.C. was roaming at will, and one of her teammates had caught fire and was setting the ball up for her taller friend. I'd rarely blocked against anyone who had the kind of height advantage B.C. had over me. And it wasn't just her height. It was her quickness and her misdirection.

She'd go up facing one way and then swivel midway through her arm swing and angle the spike. I've been known to grunt when I smash the ball, but this woman's noises were incredible. And she kept up a steady stream of abuse at the ball, at her teammates, and at me whenever I faced her across the net.

Bad move on her part. It made me jump higher. Spike harder. I killed a ball right down the line, pretty as a pro shot, and I could hear her hiss like a kettle ready to steam.

The second game went 15–12, far from a rout. Kristy gave us a pep talk cum warning to finish them off in the third game. If any of their other players woke up, we could be in trouble. B.C. was playing a hell of a game, and there was further speculation about the Olympic scout. Joy thought she might have seen him on TV. Didn't he play for the Patriots?

We had the third game won when it happened, and I'm not saying B.C. did it on purpose. But she did have that unbelievable control, and I wouldn't have put it past her, not the way she was yelling and fuming and swearing. The referee glanced over from time to time, and I think he should have called an unsportsmanlike on her, but nobody asked me.

Anyway, we needed two more points for the match. Kristy was serving on a hot streak, five points in, aiming 'em at the little fireplug who surprised everybody by setting one up. B.C. came roaring over to smash it. I countered to block her and launched myself at the same time she took off. She saw me rise to meet her, rearranged herself to fire off to my right, to miss my block entirely. Joy, next to me, moved late, and the ball would have sailed by her for the kill.

Instead of taking the easy shot, getting the side-out and the ball, B.C. switched in midair. I swear I could see

98

her eyes flicker when she decided to do it. She must have sensed that I'd relaxed, seeing that the ball was going to be Joy's to hit or miss, not mine. She didn't aim for air; she aimed for me.

On pure reflex I deflected the ball with my left hand, but it still hit my face with hardly any of its momentum gone. Then I was on the floor, crouched on knee pads and elbows, blood pooling in front of me. There was a lot of it, and it seemed like it must have come from somebody else. For a moment I flashed on the scene in the Fens and almost lost my breakfast.

Somebody thrust a towel at me and I held it to my face. It came away bright crimson.

Shit, I thought. Not my damn nose. Not again.

Kristy was yelling at the referee and at B.C. The ref was trying to get everybody back in the game.

One of the differences between men's and women's teams is how they react to injury. You watch a football game, a hockey game, and some guy gets injured, flat on his back, down for the count. The other guys on the team don't even go over to ask if he's alive. The coach comes out, the trainer, then the ambulance crew with the stretcher. With as little fuss as possible, the guy is carted off, a replacement comes in, and play resumes.

With us, if somebody takes a bad fall, stays on the parquet too long, we stop. We all rush over and offer assistance, a kind word, a hand up. A wet towel. The game stops dead until we're sure she's okay.

I prefer it. Maybe that's why you don't see many women's team sports on the tube. Takes up too much time, all that helping the wounded.

I couldn't feel the bridge of my nose. I badly wanted a mirror. The thought of the locker-room mirrors did nothing for me. If I bent down far enough to look in one, I was sure I'd get nauseated.

Two people, I think it was Edna on one side and Kristy on the other, helped me over to the bench. I sat and bloodied the towel some more. As soon as my eyes started focusing, I assured my teammates I was okay. Kristy looked at the relative size of my pupils, then asked me the key questions: What's your name? Where are you? I must have answered correctly because she motioned to our best bench-warmer.

"We won't need you for these last two points," she said. "Hit the locker room. Lie down. We'll be there in a minute."

"Yeah," I said.

As soon as the game started up again, I hauled myself to my feet. I remembered seeing a ladies' room right outside the double gym doors, one that might have a mirror in an accessible position.

It's not that I'm vain, but my nose has had its troubles. I broke it for the first time when I was six years old. My next-door neighbor had done the honors, wielding a wooden toy hammer. I busted it again when I was a cop. And cab driving did it the third time. I don't have a huge nose or anything, but the bridge has a rather distinctive bump. I've gotten fond of that bump.

I touched it as I walked. If it was broken, it wasn't a bad break. My nose wasn't squashed to one side or anything. My cheekbone hurt.

The ladies' room was where I remembered it, across from a men's room with a drinking fountain in between. The hunk was standing by the fountain holding a wet towel. He walked over and held it out to me.

"You ought to get cold water on that, Ms. Carlyle," he said. "Ice cubes would be better."

His eyes were blue.

I took the sopping towel and held it to my face. Water dripped down the front of my already sweat-soaked top. I must have been a little hazy, because I was wondering why an Olympic scout would know my name.

His voice was baritone. Accent from the South. Close up he looked even better than from afar.

I mumbled my thanks and stumbled into the bathroom. I no longer felt nauseated. From practice, I knew what to do next. I filled the sink with cold water, took a deep breath, pleased that my nose still functioned, and plunged my whole head into the sink.

The water was pink when I came up for air. I let the pink water drain and started again. This time I dared to glance in the mirror.

Not bad. I'd envisioned a hunk of raw meat, and what I saw still had the definite contours of my nose. I tried a profile view, ran my fingers carefully along the bridge. I didn't think the damn thing was even busted. I put my nose and face back in the sink. The water changed color less.

The hunk was waiting when I emerged, damp but feeling a hell of a lot better. I headed to the gym, thinking I might be able to play if we'd lost the third game, thinking I'd like a chance to spike a ball into that damned B.C. dropout.

"Ms. Carlyle, could we talk awhile?"

"Huh?" I said.

"About Manuela Estefan?"

I stopped dead. "Who are you?"

"INS."

Well, damn, I thought, who woulda guessed?

101

16

"Where'd you go? You see that last point?" Edna asked breathlessly as soon as I walked into the locker room.

Nobody needed to tell me we'd won. A winning locker room feels different from a losing one. Besides, the suburban team would have needed hours to pull back from a 2–1 deficit.

"Who's the hunk?" This from Joy. I wondered how she'd been able to see through closed doors. Probably noticed both of us disappear from the gym at the same time. The rest was pure guesswork.

I grinned at her, assured them all that I was feeling better, showered, and dressed quickly. The hunk was waiting when I came out. Joy and Edna passed while I was talking to him and gave me the eye.

"You carrying some ID?" I asked him. He yanked a brown folder like Jamieson's out of his hip pocket. It said I was speaking to Special Agent Harrison Clinton.

"Harry will do," he said with a smile that warmed up his eyes.

"You have a car, Harry?" I asked.

"Yeah."

"Mind driving me home?"

He stared at my nose. The bleeding had stopped, but I was carrying a damp towel, pressing it against my nose

103

and cheek except when conversation required removing it. Might as well keep the swelling down.

"How about to a hospital?" he suggested.

"Home," I said firmly. I wanted to know if he knew where I lived. I wanted to see if he drove a white Aries. Also, I just plain wanted to get home. I had a headache coming on that was going to be spectacular. I could feel it rumbling behind my eyes like far-off thunder on a summer afternoon.

He drove a boxy sedan, but it wasn't an Aries. I bet it was a rental or an agency job. He'd parked it in an alley behind the Y, ignoring the no-parking signs.

"You sure you don't want to make a stop at a doctor's?" he inquired when I'd belted myself into the passenger seat.

I asked him bluntly if he'd been following me around in a white Aries. It may have been rude, but his solicitousness was starting to get on my nerves.

"Not me," he said quickly.

"What about your buddy Jamieson?"

He smiled when I said the name, the corners of his eyes crinkling. He was at least my age. His skin had a weathered look you don't find much in Boston. "I'm not saying he did, but old Walter never could tail worth a damn."

"Whereas if you'd been following me, I wouldn't have caught on?" I said, raising an eyebrow skeptically.

"Well, I'm not bragging . . ." He had an easy grin over a mouthful of nicely spaced, slightly yellowed teeth. Maybe a former smoker, like me. The teeth saved him from looking like a male model. I mean, who wants perfection?

I locked my door and settled back, leaning to my right so I could watch him drive. Good cop, bad cop, was probably the name of this game. Jamieson had been nasty for no particular reason, and now Clinton had been sent to charm the details out of me. The hell with it, let him try. My head pounded faintly. I put the towel to my nose and leaned back against the headrest.

He eased the car out onto Huntington Avenue. The afternoon traffic was light.

"I wanted to tell you we appreciate your cooperation on this case," he said. "You didn't have to come forward."

I didn't respond. He took a left onto Mass. Ave., intimidating a battered pickup truck. He drove well, big hands easy on the wheel.

"Uh, I was wondering," he said after working his way through the traffic lights between Symphony Hall and the Mother Church, "do you have any idea why the Estefan woman came to you in the first place?" He'd decided to go straight up Mass. Ave. into Cambridge. I would have gone through the Fenway, taken Park Drive to Memorial Drive. Faster.

"Nope," I offered from behind my towel mask. "No idea."

"Have you handled any other cases for immigrants? It doesn't have to be in the recent past. Go back ten years if you have to."

He turned and saw my smile and looked embarrassed. "I don't suppose you could go back ten years as a private investigator, could you?"

"Ten years ago I was a cop," I said. A rookie, but I didn't tell him that.

"Hard to believe," he said with a flirtatious grin. I sat back and waited for the rest of the show.

"Ten years ago," he said after beating out a green Chevette at a traffic light. "That's about when I started."

I raised my eyebrow again. It's something I work on from time to time.

"Yep," he said, "I guess I thought I'd be out welcoming Russian defectors. Big-time undercover stuff. Berlin. Intrigue."

"You into intrigue?" I asked. "That how you knew where to find me today?"

"Wasn't too hard," he said smugly. "Just flashed my ID at that little gal lives at your place, the one with the, uh, weird hair." I knew what he'd been about to say before he substituted the line about the hair. Roz has other attributes that men, in particular, seem to notice.

"So immigration hasn't lived up to expectations?" I said, leading him on. As long as he talked, I didn't have to.

He stopped at a traffic light and swiveled to face me. "I'm not into chasing some poor OTM wants to come in here and earn food money doing the kind of shitwork native-born Americans won't touch. I want you to know that."

"OTM?" I said. It sounded familiar, but I thought I might be reacting to ATM, automated teller machines.

"Other Than Mexican," he said. "It's a category we use."

"Gotta have labels," I said dryly.

"It's for Latins only. Like, you wouldn't be an OTM." He flashed the grin at me again. He was good. It may have been the headache, but I almost felt I could trust him, that I could pour out my worries.

"Okay," I said, catching myself, "why does INS give a damn what I'm doing? Why do you care about any Manuela Estefan? There's a green card on her, right? She's legal."

He zipped past a slow Buick. "You think that's all we do, right? Round 'em up and head 'em the hell back to the border?"

"Yeah," I said, "that's what I hear you do."

"Well," he said, "that ain't all there is."

I remembered what Marian Rutledge, the Cambridge Legal Collective lawyer, had told me. "I hear you guys run detention camps on the Texas border. I hear a lot that makes me wonder why somebody who doesn't like chasing Third World poor people out of the country wouldn't maybe find other work," I said.

That shut down conversation for a while. We made it over the Harvard Bridge without causing its collapse.

"What we've got," he said in a sorrowful tone, "is one hell of a public-relations problem. And somehow I don't think Congress is gonna fund us an ad campaign."

I smiled in spite of myself. He played hurt so well. It could have been the twang. I wondered if my outburst was due to the fact that I felt attracted to the guy. Automatic self-preservation. I have a history of liking the wrong guys. When I feel the old chemistry churn, I know I've met either a much-married man or a guy who'll mess up my head. So I get argumentative right off.

He wasn't wearing a wedding band.

There was road construction in Central Square. Every bump jarred my head.

"Sure you're okay?" he said.

Behind us, somebody blared his horn.

"Fine," I said through gritted teeth.

I had the towel up to my face. He reached over and pulled a few strands of my hair free of the cloth. His hand brushed my cheek and the cynical part of me wondered if this was part of the good-cop routine. The rest of me felt the tingle.

He didn't ask for directions to the house. He didn't need them. When he pulled up in the driveway, I had my hand on the door handle, my good-bye in my mouth, but he leaned over and put a restraining hand on my arm.

"I'll level with you," he said. "What we think is going on is this: We think this Manuela Estefan was involved in some very heavy-duty stuff. Fingering folks."

"Fingering?"

"She moves around a lot. And where she moves, folks die."

"You're gonna have to tell me more than that."

"She was from El Salvador."

"Yeah." I wished he'd hurry. My head was pounding harder.

"A lot of political folks coming from El Salvador, seeking asylum and all that good stuff."

"Not that you guys let them in."

"A lot of the claims are frivolous," he said.

"Frivolous. I like that word. Frivolous, as in I'm starving to death where I live?"

"You can't get political asylum for starvation. And I don't want to argue with you. I shouldn't even be telling you this—"

"Wait up. Are you saying that Manuela, whoever she is, was pointing out people for Salvadoran death-squad hits?"

"You know what a coyote is?"

"I assume you're not talking about the animal," I said.

"A sort of animal," he continued with distaste. "A coyote is a guide, somebody who takes illegals' money and lies to them about how easy it is to get into the country, and takes a group up here, sometimes with false papers, sometimes with nothing, and strands them someplace. A few fall between the cracks, get into the country and manage to stay, but most get caught and deported."

"So?" I said.

"We've heard rumors about a female coyote named Manuela Estefan. She knows where a lot of political people wound up, what cities they're in, what contacts they've made. And, word is, she's selling that information to the highest bidder. And believe me, the INS is never the highest bidder."

I remembered Mooney's warning about death squads. I considered my Manuela, my client with the cheap shoes, the work-worn hands, and the hundred-dollar bills. I tried to imagine her as this coyote, this predator. It turned the whole picture upside down. True, my client may have lied about her name, but lying about a name doesn't rate as a mortal sin. It's not in the same league as pointing out victims to assassins.

Maybe my client was one of "Manuela's" victims, a political refugee fingered by her former guide.

"Is the Manuela with the card, this coyote Manuela, still alive?" I asked.

"We don't know," the INS man said, "but I'm concerned—we're concerned about this ad you put in the paper."

I'd forgotten about the ad. I kept that carefully off my face.

"Yeah," I said. "Well, I placed that while she—while my client —was alive."

"I know you didn't realize what you were letting yourself in for," he said, "but you've gotta back off. These guys the Estefan woman's playing with are not nice people. We've been trying to round 'em up for years now. They kill folks. Don't think twice about it."

"Is that why you're following me?"

"Don't you see, dammit, if somebody's following you, we need to know about it, because somebody might think this damn woman told you something that's going to help us."

"Then by sitting here with me, out in the open, you're setting me up, right?"

"Shit," he said. "Is everything an argument with you? Setting you up? You're doing a hell of a job by yourself, taking out an ad in the paper."

I gave up on my nose and pressed the towel to my head. "What do you want?"

"If you hear from anybody who says they want to chat with you about Manuela, you call me, okay? Not after you meet them, because there may not be any afterward, but before you meet. And I'll go with you." He handed over a card. "This number ought to get me anytime."

"Why don't you just follow me around?"

"It's not my style," he said angrily. "Look, you want to target yourself, you go ahead." His voice softened abruptly. "But I'd hate for anything to happen to a lady with hair the color of yours, you know. I hardly ever see hair that color."

"They let Jamieson work the men and you work the women?"

"Usually." He smiled with just the right amount of self-deprecation. "They slipped up with Jamieson earlier. Didn't know you were gonna be you."

"And now you know."

The Southern accent got heavier. "Ma'am, it'll be a pleasure keeping an eye on you."

"Don't count on it," I said.

He reached over and put his hand on my arm, just below the elbow. "Get some ice on that nose, take two aspirin, and lie down," he said. "Call me in the morning?"

Somehow I fumbled the locks and got in the house. As I slammed the door the headache throbbed into full flower, and pain washed over me, leaving me momentarily weak, clinging to the banister. Where he'd touched it, my arm felt hot.

17

Sunday passed. That's the best I can say for it. I spent it with my nose packed in ice, downing aspirin every four hours. My nose didn't swell much, but my head felt like a balloon. Monday morning I decided I'd live.

Rupert Murdoch likes to call the site of his publishing empire One Herald Square, but it's plain old 300 Harrison Avenue to me, one more impossible place to park. Exasperated after a ten-minute search, I plunked the Toyota in a loading zone and prayed the visit to the classified ads department wouldn't take long.

Imagine my delight as I stood and tapped a foot and waited till my presence was acknowledged by a teenybop secretary puffing on a cigarette, adjusting a high heel, and chatting on the phone as if she had no intention of ever signing off. She seemed hyperactive, maybe on speed, with her jaw, hands, feet, and hips in overdrive. I almost developed a tic waiting for her to get off the phone.

At least I wouldn't have to look for parking near the *Globe* building too. I'd phoned. They hadn't received any responses to my ad. The *Herald* had one.

She finally said farewell and teetered in my direction. Some women can't walk in heels and shouldn't try. They look so goddamned vulnerable. If I were a purse snatcher, I'd go after ladies in five-inch spikes. I gave her the box number from my ad and she pulled one lone envelope out of a wooden grid. It didn't have a stamp on it.

"Somebody bring this in?" I asked.

"I dunno," she said. It was an automated response. If I'd asked her the time, the day of the week, her mother's maiden name, she'd have mumbled "I dunno" in syllables of sheer indifference. She had the glazed look of a late-night partygoer.

I took a twenty out of my wallet. Enough to pay for a manicure for her blood-red talons. Her eyes got interested. "Were you here when this came in?" I asked, holding up the envelope and keeping my fingers firmly on the twenty.

"Oooh," she said with a quick grin, "might have been."

" 'Might have been' isn't good enough," I said.

"What if I said a Spanish lady brought it in, kind of dumpy, maybe twenty, wearing a flower-print dress?"

"I'd say you keep your eyes open."

"Got to do something to keep from catching brain death in this place," she said with a sniff. Maybe the bash last night had included a little powder snorting. I wondered if the lady had gone home to change or come straight to work from the party. Her purple satin tank top and short black skirt weren't really suited to office air-conditioning. I couldn't tell if her eye makeup was badly smudged or meant to be that way.

"When did the lady bring it by?"

"She was waiting when I opened up at nine. She didn't speak good English, but she had the paper and she pointed to the ad, so I got the box number and stuck it in. I didn't get her fingerprints or anything."

If she didn't speak English, I wondered how she'd read the ad in the first place.

"Notice anything else? Jewelry? Hair?"

"It was early, you know. Real early," the secretary said with a yawn.

The phone rang and the young woman cursed. I gave her the twenty and my card.

"If you remember anything else—"

"Don't count on it," she said, one hand on the phone.

"What's your name?"

"Helen," she said. "Like Troy."

She still hadn't picked up the phone when I left. I wondered if she would.

I didn't read the note until I was back in my car. Once behind the wheel, I slit the envelope with a nail file and pulled out a sheet of unremarkable white paper. Three words, that's all. In pencil, written by a shaky hand, or a hand tracing unfamiliar letters: Hunneman Pillow Factory.

I let out my breath and realized I'd been holding it. I punched on the tape deck and smothered a laugh. That happens to me a lot. I'm expecting a note that says "Meet me under the Harvard Bridge at midnight" and instead I get one directing me to a pillow factory.

18

A pillow factory. I imagined clouds of white goose down. Just thinking about pillow factories made me sleepy, so I kept careful watch in my rearview mirror. Nobody tailed me to the corner drugstore, where I checked out Hunneman Pillows in the phone booth Yellow Pages. I scratched down the Brighton address on the back of an envelope. Nobody tailed me from the drugstore to Cambridge Street.

I turned the volume up on the tape deck and sang along with Chris Smither on "Love You Like a Man." Bonnie Raitt covers it, but I have a fondness for the original raunchy version.

> Those men you been seein' got their balls up on the shelf,
> You know they can never love you, babe,
> They can't even love themselves.
> If you need someone who can, I could be your lover man,
> You better believe me when I tell you,
> I could love you like a man.

The lyrics made me think about the INS guy, not Walter Jamieson, the shriveled-up rat, but the second guy, Harry Clinton, the one with the eyes and the shoulders.

Uh-huh, I thought, checking around for a white Aries.

Sam Gianelli's been in Italy a damn long time. And what's he been doing in those Turin hotel rooms with the big canopied beds? Dreaming of me?

Mississippi John Hurt sings my all-time favorite blues rhyme.

> Red rooster say: Cock-a-doodle-do,
> Richland woman say: Any dude'll do.

I'm not like that Richland woman, I told myself virtuously. But Harry Clinton was on my mind.

Hunneman Pillows was located off North Beacon Street in between a plumbing-supply shop and a going-out-of-business shoe-factory outlet. As far as I can figure, North Beacon Street has no relationship to Beacon Street at all and is just called that to throw new cabbies off the scent.

Veteran jockey that I am, I wasn't fooled.

The Hunneman factory seemed to be an unmarked brick square with patches of boarded-up window and an air of desertion. It was plunked next to a slab of pot-holed cement that could have been a parking lot or an auto junkyard. It didn't have any neat yellow lines delineating spaces, but it did have lots of junky cars. I found most of an empty slot for my Toyota, squeezing between a rusted Oldsmobile and a maroon Chevy with a battered left rear fender. I took in a deep breath and eased my body out the door with maybe a quarter inch to spare. If I'd been wearing looser jeans, I'd never have made it.

The white Aries wasn't in the lot.

Hunneman didn't exactly advertise its presence. There was no sign over the door, no billboard. I checked the address I'd scrawled on the envelope. Without it, I'd have driven right by. With it, I wondered if the factory had closed down and moved out.

I leaned against the hood of an old Ford wagon, pulled Harry Clinton's card out of my pocket, and stared at the phone number until it blurred before my eyes.

I figured I should call Mooney. And Harry Clinton. I got back in my car and sat, ignition keys weighing down my hand.

Mooney was pursuing some wacko serial killer. I realized I had trouble believing in his existence. Oh, I'm not naïve, I know the goons are out there. I read about them in the papers like everybody else, glued to the print by the horror, unable to look away. But I don't see them here, in my city. Despite the Boston Strangler, I think of them as California crazies, Texas loners. Far away. Other.

I wasn't concerned with a serial killer. I was concerned with a woman who'd worn a filigree ring, who'd paid me five hundred dollars to get her a green card that didn't even belong to her.

Why?

I tried to make my client's visit fit with Harry Clinton's theory. If my Manuela was searching for his Manuela, the turncoat coyote, could that make my Manuela a member of a so-called death squad? If so, why the hell had she turned up dead herself?

I decided not to call Clinton. Still, I wasn't ready to rush the factory's front door and demand to see Manuela Estefan.

I checked out my nose in the rearview mirror. It was tender to the touch but not broken, I thought. There was some bruising high on my right cheek.

Damn. I could sit here all day watching my cheek turn color or I could stop dithering and check out a goddamn lead. I slid out of the car and walked resolutely toward the factory.

I gave a door a push. I wasn't sure if it was the front door, the back door, the servants' entrance, or what. Locked. There was a doorbell to the right of the brass handle. I pushed it, and after a three-minute wait during which I pounded on the metal surface, a buzzer buzzed. The lock clicked open and I breezed on through.

Noise, light—and different, thicker air. Those were the things that got to me, even in the vestibule. The lighting was awful, dim flickering fluorescents. The noise, a conveyor-belt-type racheting, was worse. And the air—I clamped my mouth shut, but then I had to breathe through my nose and smell the damp burned-rubbery aroma. I opened my mouth and thought maybe this was what New Yorkers talked about when they mentioned air you could taste, what L.A. dwellers dealt with when the air turned to yellow smog.

Had they had a fire here? Did it smell like this all the time? I could see three women shoehorned into a cubicle office, typing and chattering, not calling for help. The atmosphere must seem normal to them. I licked my lips and rubbed my mouth. I could feel something cottony on the back of my hand.

The women were conversing in animated Spanish, but they froze when I approached, like startled deer poised to flee. I yelled *"¡Buenas días!"* loud enough to make myself heard over the machinery, but that didn't seem to reassure them. They shot anxious looks at each other. I studied them, checking for my dumpy informant in her flowered dress.

A phone rang. The oldest of the three, who must have been all of twenty-five, picked up a dusty receiver from her cluttered desk and answered in an accented voice. She directed the call to Mr. Hunneman, pressing buttons on a console and hanging up with a loud bang, as if she'd once been accused of eavesdropping.

One of the women probably would have said something to me sooner or later, I guess, but they were saved by the arrival of a guy. A big guy.

"You ring the bell?" His voice was a low growl that carried.

"Yeah." He wasn't any taller than I am, but he must have outweighed me by a hundred pounds. A lot of it was stomach, but some of it was muscle. He wore a once-white T-shirt with a Coors Beer logo. It didn't quite meet a massive silver belt buckle but tucked easily into his jeans in back. It was just his belly that protruded.

"No soliciting," he half hollered over the throb of the conveyor belt.

My eyebrows inched up. He looked like the kind of guy who only knew one meaning for *soliciting,* and I haven't been accused of that since my police department undercover hooker nights. I smiled in spite of myself.

"I'm not selling anything," I yelled. "I'm here to see Mr. Hunneman." Since he was taking phone calls, I figured he must be somewhere in the vicinity.

"Oh, yeah?" Beer Belly said. He seemed amused.

"Yes," I said politely. "Which way to his office?"

"What's this all about?"

"I'll tell Mr. Hunneman when I see him," I said, keeping a set smile on my face.

"You tell me or you won't get to see anybody," the fat man declared. He took a step forward.

"It's about a job," I said, lowering my eyelashes and making it sound like employment was the furthest thing from my mind. Maybe he'd let me pass if he thought I was some fling his boss had going on the side.

119

"For you?" His smile broadened. He was missing a tooth.

I indicated the Hispanic women, who stopped all activity and gazed at me wide-eyed. "Maybe one of them could tell him I'd like to see him, check if he's too busy, you know."

"He's busy," Beer Belly said flatly.

I cursed inwardly. My coloring eliminated any chance of passing for Hispanic, but I should have faked an Irish accent. My dad was half Irish, and we used to kid each other in hokey overdone brogues. This jerk might have bought the tale if I'd come on like an illegal immigrant.

"I won't take up much of his time," I promised.

"Who wants to see me? Why didn't anybody call?" The voice was tenor, but the man was large: broad-shouldered, barrel-chested, with legs a bit short for his girth. Otherwise he'd have towered over me instead of topping out at six feet. He had the florid complexion of a heavy drinker. His reddish-blond hair was fine and a little frizzy, like misplaced baby hair. His features were regular—far-apart eyes, wide bridge to his nose—blurred a little by extra weight. Twenty pounds lighter and he'd have been a very handsome man.

His tone was good-natured, but there was strain behind it, wariness.

Beer Belly seemed struck dumb by Hunneman's sudden appearance, which gave me a chance to get in the first word.

I stuck out my hand eagerly. "Pleased to meet you, sir," I said. I've found a little respectfulness can generally get you an audience with anybody short of the Pope.

"She says she's looking for work," Beer Belly chimed in.

120

Hunneman stopped mid-stride. He turned his eyes on me, gave me a thorough exam that made me feel naked. I got the feeling there was more than sexual interest in his glance. "Oh," he said carefully, lightly, "and how did you hear about us?"

"A friend," I said, matching his casual tone. "She said you needed a secretary. I'm a great secretary. Dorothy Gibbs. Not my name, I went to school there. Practically got my certificate, but then I got the flu. Real bummer, you know?"

"Who's your friend?" Hunneman asked with a charming smile. He wore a well-cut navy business suit that would have looked fine in a bank or a boardroom. It seemed pretty formal compared to the fat man's T-shirt. Cuff links gleamed at his wrists, gold or brass.

"She make a mistake?" I asked. "Maybe I misunderstood her."

"I don't need a secretary," Hunneman said.

"Too bad. I'm good at shorthand, and I can run a computer and everything."

"Your friend work here?" Hunneman walked into the tiny office. The three women busied themselves filing papers and typing, faces set, eyes downcast.

I watched Hunneman and I had the feeling that the Coors man was watching me just as avidly. The factory owner's suit looked expensive; so did his highly polished black loafers.

"What's your friend's name?" Hunneman snatched up some papers from a desk. He wore a domed ring on his left hand. High school or college, not a wedding ring.

I didn't want to part with Manuela's name. Not yet.

"Hey, what difference does it make?" I said cheerfully. "Her English isn't so hot, and I probably misunderstood her, like I said."

121

"No difference." Hunneman came up beside me, stood a little too close. He had a few reddish-gold hairs on his upper lip. "I thought maybe you'd like to stop in and say hello to her, that's all."

Sure, I thought. But I pretended to give his suggestion some consideration before turning it down. He smiled at me, but his eyes stayed cool and remote. I thought he might be wearing cologne, but in the poisonous atmosphere I couldn't be sure. His eyes were slate-colored, like a winter sky.

"Sorry to take up your time," I said.

"No problem," he answered. He nodded to Beer Belly. "Show her out."

I opened my mouth to protest that I could find my own way to the door, but I was interrupted by a deafening whistle. The narrow corridor filled with women heading toward the door in quick, grim march-step. They didn't speak. Most of them had handkerchief triangles tied across their mouths like bad men in old Westerns.

Hunneman disappeared through a doorway beyond the secretarial cubicle. The fat man said, "Outside, okay?"

He took a step toward me, and since he blocked the whole corridor, I didn't see that I had a lot of choices. I nodded and joined the flow, towering over the women, sidestepping outside the front door, no longer part of the parade. An observer.

As they stepped out the door the women loosened their masks, a few whipping them off over their heads, some going to the trouble of untying, balancing handbags precariously while they used both hands for the maneuver. The majority just pulled the masks down over their faces until they turned into neck scarves.

Most of them coughed and snorted at their first breath of real air.

The faces seemed predominantly Hispanic, but there was a sprinkling of fair hair and freckles, as well as a contingent of dark-skinned women who seemed to crowd together.

Which of them had come to the *Herald* this morning with the message? I stared at them, searching for a twentyish, dumpy woman in a flowered dress.

A face jumped out of the crowd.

Marta inched along slowly, minus her cane, leaning on the arm of another woman, a woman who looked like her in a vague, familial way. Cousin Lilia.

So Marta didn't know my Manuela.

Maybe my anger beamed across the driveway. Marta glanced over suddenly, caught my eye. Her face turned pale and she stumbled. She murmured something to her cousin, kept her gaze fixed on the broken concrete. Lilia turned back to the factory door to see if they'd been observed, to see if someone was watching me.

Marta wasn't embarrassed at being caught in any lie. She was scared. Plain scared.

She walked right by me, still staring at the ground, her back unnaturally straight. She seemed to be holding her breath.

I pretended not to know her, giving all the women the same careful scrutiny. I noticed the Coors T-shirt framed in the doorway. Was Marta afraid of the fat man?

I'd mentioned my "friend" inside. Now I looked from face to face, as if I couldn't spot her. I glanced at my watch, tapped my foot, acted out my impatience in mime. Maybe this wasn't her shift. Well, I'd give it a few more minutes, see if she came out. Be nice to say hello, but no big deal if this was her day off.

I waited until all the women came out, the last few rushing to keep up with the crowd. Beer Belly watched me from the doorway. I was afraid I might have reacted involuntarily when I saw Marta, so I decided to spread the suspicion around. I asked a fat lady of fifty if she knew a woman named Hester Prynne. I asked a tiny redhead and a black girl of no more than sixteen the same question.

They gave me curt, negative shakes of their heads, kept on walking.

They were all scared of me.

19

I found a space at the curb two blocks from Marta's project. I quickly locked up, ignoring the RESIDENT PARKING ONLY warning again, and practically ran to Marta's door. I didn't want her to climb the steps twice, and I figured she probably had the smarts to realize I'd be right behind her and wait for me in the vestibule. Waiting in the vestibule of a place like hers could get you mugged or worse, so I hurried.

She was inside the front door, breathing hard, seated on the steps. She hauled herself up by the banister when I knocked.

I didn't bother with hello, just blurted out, "That woman I asked you about, the one who called herself Manuela Estefan. You told her about me."

"*Hablemos*—" she began, and then stopped when she realized my Spanish wouldn't be up to it. "We talk upstairs." She coughed a couple of times, and it shook her whole body. I helped her with the stairs.

"You heard anything about getting a ground-floor place?" I asked, my voice tight with anger. I wanted to rain questions on her, but I had to admit she was right. It was a conversation that ought to take place behind closed doors.

She replied with bitter resignation, "There is a list." I mean, what can you do if there's a list?

Goddamn the housing authority for putting a woman with bad arthritis up a flight of steps. And damn Marta for not trusting me.

"Why did you send her to me?" I asked as soon as we got to Marta's door. There was nobody around, and I couldn't take the silence any longer. Wordlessly Marta handed me her keys so I could work the locks. Inside, there was no noise from Paolina's room, no response when Marta called out her name.

"I didn't send you nobody," Marta said wearily, sinking into the chair in front of the TV. "Bring me a glass of water, no?"

I sighed and brought her water from the kitchen, running it for a long time, thinking about lead pipes and chemical residue and bottled water.

When I got back to the living room, damned if she hadn't turned on the set. I punched the off button and stood in front of the screen. "Somebody told me today that Manuela Estefan worked at the Hunneman Pillow Factory, had something to do with the pillow factory. So I go there and you and Lilia march out the door. That's a coincidence?"

"*No comprendo* 'coinci'—"

"Come on, Marta, spare me the *no comprendo* crap."

"Okay, sit down, I tell you this. I don't know the name Manuela. I don't know no names. That place is a place where people don't got no names, no faces, just hands to work with. I work there just a little while, just some days. I don't know no Manuela."

"Maybe she had another name there. Maybe Aurelia, Aurelia Gaitan."

"That name I don't know either. And I never talk

126

about you—" She bit her bottom lip and stopped abruptly. "No, I'm a liar, maybe I did. Maybe I show off your card. Maybe when I'm there, I talk too much and somebody hears."

"Hears what?"

She took a long drink of water, coughed, drank again. "I talk, you know. Maybe I say there's this Anglo woman who's nice to my daughter. A woman lives alone like a man and helps people, who don't think I'm so stupid 'cause I don't *hablo perfecto inglés.*"

"You're not stupid. I know it, so don't try to pull any fast ones on me."

"Talk to the Welfare. They think I'm stupid. The men at the factory, they think I'm *muy estúpida.* All the women are stupid."

"You don't have to work in a place like that, Marta."

"No?" she said, her fingers playing nervously on the armrest. "And my sons don't have to go to school, either, no? Let them be janitors, pick up Anglo trash the rest of their lives."

And your daughter, I wanted to scream. What about her?

But I held my tongue. It's an old battle in a long war. If Paolina wants to go to college, I'll pay her way. Marta sees no use in it.

She acted as if she could hear my thoughts.

"Paolina should be at home," she said fretfully. "I should make the girl come home after school and do the housework. Look at this place, this house for pigs. In the school they teach her to make stupid gold fishes, not bread, not stew. She shouldn't be staying after school for the band, for the play. Soon she is old enough to quit."

"If she wants to," I said.

127

"If I want her to. Remember that. She is my daughter and she does what I say."

Sometimes there's no talking to Marta. If we were going to have an argument today, I didn't want it to center on Paolina.

"You hungry?" I asked.

"If the girl isn't home, there's nothing in the house. She's supposed to go to the store, get rice, food. But she stays at the school, don't do nothing."

"I could make you some tea. Some coffee?"

"Coffee would be nice," she admitted.

There was enough instant in a small jar in a grime-smeared cupboard to make one decent cup or two weak ones. I made Marta's strong, the way she likes it, and filled my cup with water from the tap. I probably won't die from Cambridge water.

"So maybe you said something about me at work," I ventured when I came back balancing the two cups. That wouldn't account for the business card I'd seen my Manuela tuck away in her handbag.

I'd placed two sugar cubes on the saucer. Marta put a cube in her mouth, between her teeth, and sipped the coffee through it. My mom used to drink it that way.

"Yeah," she said. "I don't remember, but we talk to pass the time."

Shout is what they'd have to do over the din of that machinery.

"Tell me about the factory," I said. "Tell me how you got the job."

"You gonna tell the Welfare I'm working?"

"Oh, yeah, Marta, you know me. I'm a blabbermouth, tell everything I know to the government."

That won a grudging smile. One sugar cube was completely melted away. She toyed with the other one on the

128

saucer. "Lilia," she said. "Lilia tells me about it. They ask no questions."

"What do you mean, no questions?"

"You work, you get paid. Cash money. You don't gotta fill in no forms. And 'cause of Lilia, 'cause she works regular, they let me work sometimes when I feel okay."

"Like today?" It was pretty damn obvious she didn't feel all right.

"Or when I need money," she said, staring down at the cracked tile.

"When you need money, I can help you out."

She flared up. "I don't mind work."

"It's just that the factory didn't look like the easiest place to work in," I said soothingly.

"Is noisy, *sí*. Always the machinery. You wouldn't think to lift a lot of feathers would be so heavy. Hurt my back some. Is no so bad. If my fingers are better, like before this damn arthritis, I could sew the pillows. Is more easy."

"They pay okay?"

She shrugged. "Okay."

"What does 'okay' mean in dollars and cents?"

"Two ninety-five the hour."

"Christ, Marta," I protested. "That's way below minimum wage."

"They gotta give some of the money to the government."

"Sure," I said, "especially if you don't fill in any forms."

"Money for bribes," she said through closed teeth, as if she were exasperated at having to repeat the facts of life for the fifth time to a slow adolescent. "They don't ask questions. They pay cash money."

"You're being treated like shit. You ought to see yourself coming out of that place, blinded, deafened, dazed. You ought to resent it. You ought to turn the bastards in. There are laws to protect you from . . ." I started on a soapbox speech but ran down like an unwound clock. My grandmother worked in a New York City sweatshop when she came to this country. Eighteen-hour days chained to a sewing machine in an unventilated hole with boarded-up windows. Once she fainted from lack of air, and the foreman shoved her aside so the machine wouldn't be idle. My grandmother joined the International Ladies Garment Workers Union, went out on strike. Once, walking a picket line, she hit a scab over the head with a protest sign. She wound up in a Bowery jail.

Other kids got fairy tales. I got union stories.

Protest! I wanted to scream at Marta. Those women should organize and protest like my grandmother did. But then, cops hadn't threatened to send Grandma back where she came from.

"Okay," I said, "I can see why you work there, but why Lilia?"

"I told you, they don't want no papers from *La Migra.*"

"Lilia's been here for years. You told me she was going to file for amnesty."

"She change her mind. She no apply. I tell her what you say, but she figure it's a way to trick her, to send her back, maybe take the children away."

I shook my head. I must have been shaking it for a while, but I suddenly realized I was shaking it—grimly, sadly. Asking to be taken advantage of, asking for it, that's what these women did. So frightened, so passive, and still not safe. "How many work there?" I asked.

"Why you wanna know?"

"How many?"

130

"Treinta, maybe. *No sé."*

We were getting more Spanish. Pretty soon Marta's English would dry up altogether.

"I saw the front door, the hallway, the little office where the three women work. Are there a lot of other rooms?"

"No sé."

"Do you all work in one big room? Come on, Marta, I need to know this."

"You gonna make trouble, tell your cop friends?"

"I don't know," I said.

"You tell them, I'm gonna be the one in trouble."

"How?"

"My own cousin, she gonna lose her work. Lilia can't work no place else. The law change. Now you have to have the papers to get a job, or the boss, he's in trouble. It cost him lots of money, maybe jail, I don't know. Lilia can't go no place else. And the women find out, they tear out my hair. Please. We need money, work."

I thought about the foul air and the noise and the pay. And Manuela.

"A woman who worked there died."

"Maybe she work there. I don't know."

"The police don't know anything about the woman. How can they find her killer if I don't tell them what I know?"

"You don't know nothing. And I tell you, if a woman is dead, it's because she got a man angry with her. You live a nice life, you don't know, maybe. Nobody kills this woman because she works stuffing feathers into pillows. It's because of something with a man. She sleeps with him, she doesn't sleep with him. Who knows? But you got no reason to make trouble for Lilia and me and all those women at the factory. You make trouble there, I can't stay here, pay the rent. I go somewhere else. With Paolina. You *comprende*?"

If I talked about the factory, she'd take my little sister away. I got the message, and I didn't like it.

"Promise me you no tell about the factory."

"Marta—"

"I mean it. You talk, I take Paolina away."

"Where would you—"

She stopped me with another rush of words. "It won't do you no good tell the police anyway. The police, they know." She leaned forward and lowered her voice, rubbed her thumb and forefingers together in the universal symbol for under-the-table graft. "The boss, he pays them money to forget. A place like that doesn't last unless money changes hands. That's what the women say."

"Who's the boss?" I asked. "Mr. Hunneman? A big guy with reddish-blond hair, well dressed?"

"I don't know. He don't come out and greet me personal when I come to work."

"The men who work there, tell me about them. Maybe one of them was sleeping with Manuela."

"The guard. The shift supervisors. The boss man I never see."

I described the big-bellied Coors T-shirt man.

"The guard," Marta said tersely. "None of the women sleeps with that son of a dog."

"What do they need a guard for?" I asked.

She shrugged. "If there's trouble, I suppose."

"Have they had trouble before?"

"Once I heard some girls make trouble about the pay, say it's not enough. Say the machinery is too noisy, the lunch break too short, and the women should stop working."

"And what happened?"

132

Marta shrugged again. "Those girls don't work there anymore. They bring in new ones. Always new ones." She took a final gulp of her coffee and held out the empty cup. "You make me another cup, no?"

"I'm sorry," I said. "That's all there is."

Her lips pressed together, whitened. "And the lazy girl is still not home. No coffee, no nothing. The girl is old enough to work, a girl so big as that. But no, she's too good to work. Like her father, she is, a liar like her father. She told you where I work, didn't she? I tell her it's a secret, but she tells you, no? Because she thinks you'd be better for a mother to her, an Anglo lady gives charity. If I lose my work, it's gonna be because she—"

"Wait a minute, Marta," I said firmly. "Paolina didn't tell me. I asked her, but she wouldn't. She listened to you."

But Marta wasn't listening to me. She went on, rapping her empty coffee cup on the chair arm by way of punctuation. "Just like her father, that girl. You can't trust her for nothing. She's never here, she's out doing God knows what with boys maybe, with strangers, while her mother sits without a cup of coffee, without a piece of bread to offer a guest."

My hand itched to slap her, to make the words stop, but they kept coming, angry words about Paolina's father, about Paolina. She was so loud, I didn't hear the footsteps on the stairs. I just heard the steps running away from the door and knew whose they must be.

By the time I got to the door and unbolted it, she was gone. I could hear the echo of the downstairs door slamming. I ran over to the window. I heard steps, but I couldn't see her running away.

"Shut up," I said to Marta.

I should have said it sooner.

133

I looked under the front stoop on the way out, even though I knew it was wasted motion. It used to be Paolina's refuge when tragedy struck. Tragedy was anything from bad grades to lost boots, but she hasn't hidden there in years.

The rotted side board had been replaced. Even if it were loose, there wouldn't have been room for Paolina to squeeze through.

I was glad of that. I remembered the scurry of rats down there. I'd never seen one, but I remembered the noise.

Maybe she'd spotted my car. Maybe I'd yank open the front door and find her sitting there. Not so easy. She couldn't be in the car, since I'd locked all the doors, and the Cambridge public schools don't teach ten-year-olds to boost cars yet, although sometimes I wonder. But maybe she'd be standing nearby.

She wasn't.

So, I told myself, she went to Lilia's or a friend's house. I decided I'd call Marta in an hour or two and find out which.

I still circled the block and made a series of passes through the project, keeping my eyes on the sidewalk, looking for her. A new Chinese take-out had opened on the corner. Two young boys with shaved heads and cropped T-shirts wrestled near a fire hydrant. I felt like I was a cop again. After a couple of months in a radio unit you stop thinking about driving and concentrate on the street. Your eyes pick out anything off, as if it were a color image smack in the middle of a black-and-white photograph.

I hadn't heard Marta mention her long-missing husband twice in three years. Why the burst of anger today? Had she heard from him? Was he in town? Was that the reason for Paolina's bizarre behavior, her shaky school attendance?

I shook off the thought. I'd ask Paolina flat out the next time we spoke. If Dad had turned up to make trouble, we'd deal with it. I'd deal with it.

I gave up and headed home. For now my job was to find out more about the pillow factory, if possible without shutting the place down. Poor Lilia. With citizenship so close, her fear had scared her off, and now she'd be working at Hunneman's Pillows with its foul air and machine-gun racket for all eternity, afraid to ask for a raise or a day off, expendable for life.

I wondered about Marta's conviction that cops were paid off to ignore Hunneman's. Marta couldn't be discounted on statements like that. She had an uncanny sense of what was going on, the kind of intuition men label "woman's" and scoff at.

My mom used to say that intuition was what slaves had and bosses never bothered to acquire. It grew from the need to please without calling attention to yourself. The slave learned to catch hidden signals, subtle signs of approval and disapproval, learned to anticipate events, to soothe tempers, to make nice.

Who took bribes? The cops, the INS, city code inspectors? All of the damned above?

By the time I reached home I'd decided. If cops were taking bribes, Mooney wasn't one of them. It's not his district, and it's not his style. So I phoned him, and of course he was out. I didn't try him at home because his mother answers the phone. Cop's widow, cop's mother, traditional Irish Catholic to the core, she disapproves of me. And she always provokes me into giving her more reasons to disapprove.

Stymied, I wandered into the kitchen and came upon Roz. What the hell she was wearing, I don't know. To tell the truth, it looked like rags. A consignment-shop special or a designer original. Probably the former. It was black, like almost everything she wears besides the T-shirts— short, tight, and, at least from the rear, definitely eye-catching, due to a highly slit skirt and a few scattered sequins. Her hair was brassy blond, which it has been before, but not yesterday. It disoriented me. I wasn't entirely sure who she was.

The smell of turpentine was reassuring. Who else would be painting in my kitchen? More to the point, who else would be painting a still life of a giant-sized can of Ajax, a moldy potato, and, yes, a rubber glove, stuffed so it looked like it was reaching for something?

I rarely comment on Roz's art. I used to, but then she'd explain the symbolism of each painting in great detail.

"Hi," I said when her paintbrush was away from canvas. Far be it from me to mess up a painting of a rubber glove fondling our Ajax.

"Yo," she said, "give me a minute to wind this up, okay?" She didn't turn around. Her attention was riveted on the label of the Ajax can.

137

Fine with me. I went over to the fridge, pulled two slices of ham out of a plastic package, used two slices of cheese for bread, stared at the clock, and called it a late lunch.

Roz laid down her brush and turned around with a satisfied sigh. "A guy came," she said.

From the front her appearance was startling. Her brassy hair had a streak of coal black starting at her part and running down one side.

She strolled over to the refrigerator and seized a jar of peanut butter, her principal diet. I don't know why she doesn't have scurvy.

"Guy have a name?" I asked.

"Guy had a bod," she said, forming her lips into a soundless whistle. "You don't want him, let me know."

"But did he have a name?"

"Clinton," she said.

"That's not a man," I said, "that's an Immigration agent."

"Look again," she advised with a grin.

"What did he want?"

"You," she said sadly. "Not me. He'll call later."

"You busy?" I asked.

She stared critically at her work. "Busy meaning what?"

"You free for a job?"

"Sure," she said.

Someday when I ask her, Roz is going to ask me what job, or how much I'll pay her, or whether it's legal or illegal, and then maybe I'll think of her as real. I don't know what I think of her as now. Some kind of phenomenon.

I sent her out to research Hunneman's, City Hall stuff —who owns it, who leases it, corporate or individual ownership, tax records. I could tell she was disappointed by the job.

"And," I added, "you might go over to the Cambridge Legal Collective. Ask for Marian Rutledge. See if she's got any clients who work at Hunneman's. Get her to search files. There's a good-looking guy secretary. Maybe you can vamp him and see if he'll find you the stuff."

"Vamp him?" she asked. "Did you really say that?"

"Forgive me," I said. "It's your dress."

"Well, I think I know what you mean," she said. "It'd depend on whether he's built."

"The important thing is who owns Hunneman's."

"I'll get it," she said.

"Be discreet."

I actually said that to somebody who looks like Roz.

21

The phone rang and I ran to get it, hoping Paolina's voice would be on the other end.

It was Kristy, trying to schedule a special volleyball practice to rev us up for Saturday's title match. I dutifully took down time and place and said I'd be there if I could arrange it. No promises.

"Nose okay?" she asked.

"Fine," I lied.

I ended the conversation before she could inquire about Harry Clinton, the Olympic scout.

I dialed Mooney's office again. This time somebody picked up his phone and said they thought he was somewhere in the building. I left a message: Don't go anywhere till you talk to Carlotta. The guy on the other end said sure, he'd tell him, but from his uninterested tone I didn't think he would.

I grabbed my handbag and ran down the front steps.

I think better when I'm driving. Part of me relaxes as soon as I settle in the driver's seat and punch on the radio. Stray thoughts line up and organize themselves in neat rows and columns.

It seemed suddenly clear to me that I needed to make a stop before visiting Mooney, and I was pulling into the

Herald driveway before I was entirely sure of the thought process that had brought me there.

I abandoned the car in a slot with a nameplate on it—some reporter's perk, I guessed. I hoped he was out on a hot story that would keep him away from the office parking lot.

Helen, the party girl who'd given me my envelope, was still on duty, if chatting on the phone qualified as on duty. I listened to what Joe did to Sue and how Sue was going to fix him good. It didn't sound like a business call. I cleared my throat. I didn't want to miss seeing Mooney because of my brainstorm.

She got off the phone and heeled her precarious way over to me. "No more mail for you," she said.

"You remember," I said. That was promising.

"For twenty bucks I remember a lot," she said.

"That's just what I want to talk to you about," I said.

On my way out of the building I saw the headline blaring from a stack of papers on some receptionist's desk. I fumbled in my bag, trying to find change.

"It's okay," the lady behind the desk said with a toothy smile. "Take one. Read the *Herald.*"

SERIAL KILLER STALKS FENS! HOW MANY DEAD?

No wonder Mooney wasn't answering his phone.

22

I knew the desk sergeant, so he gave me no hassle, just a clip-on badge that authorized me to wander the station.

Mooney was in his office, and he wasn't alone. Much to my lack of delight, Walter Jamieson was with him. I gritted my teeth, knocked, and strolled in. The air was smoke-filled, evidence of a recent meeting unless Mooney had fallen off the wagon. I inhaled deeply. I gave it up a long time ago, but I still get a rush from the secondhand stuff.

Jamieson didn't exactly snarl at me. Mooney cracked a smile, not a great smile, but an effort nonetheless. Jamieson was perched on the edge of the guest chair. Mooney sat in the chair behind the desk, and that took care of the seating facilities and most of the available space. I leaned my backside against a wall and slid down until I was practically on the floor. I used to sit like that in Mooney's office a lot.

Mooney stared at me hard, lifted his hand, and touched his cheekbone. "Want to swear out a complaint?" he asked.

So much for my attempts at bruise camouflage via makeup.

"Don't let me interrupt you," I said as Jamieson steamed.

143

"Mr. Jamieson was leaving," Mooney said pointedly.

"I was not," Jamieson denied.

"Look," Mooney said, "we're cooperating on this case, but cooperation means you file the right forms and we send you the relevant data. It does *not* mean I give you material before I get it, okay?"

From my seat on the floor I could stare up at the map on the back of the door, at the four pushpins clustered near the Fens.

Jamieson made as if to start a new wave of protest, but he kept glancing down at me and stopping. I guess he was unwilling to share his valuable thoughts with an outsider. "What is she doing here?" he finally blurted.

"Well," Mooney said, "I hope she's come to take me out to dinner. After that . . ." He gave an eloquent shrug.

Jamieson blushed and tightened his lips disapprovingly. He said, "I need copies of the reports for our files."

"I'll send them over," Mooney said.

"I'd like to take them with me," Jamieson said.

"I'll send them."

"Quit stalling me, Lieutenant."

"I can give you everything we've got in a teaspoon," Mooney said through clenched teeth. "Listen up. The FBI hasn't come up with more than fifty similar crimes yet. The medical examiner says the women were all killed in a similar manner. I gave you that hot flash before. The M.E. can't say they were killed by the same man, he can't say not by the same man. I can tell you they were killed by the same man. How do I know? With my gut. We're going through mountains of missing-persons reports, from Kansas City, from Oregon, for chrissake, but so far we got no matches."

Jamieson consulted a small wire-ringed notebook. "Were the women raped?" he asked.

144

Mooney shrugged his shoulders.

"Drugs?"

"No evidence."

"How did the killer get the body from that apartment to the park? Without anybody seeing him?"

"He's lucky and smart. The FBI's got a word for these guys. They call them 'organized' killers, and they're a bitch to catch. There's an alleyway behind those buildings on Westland. He must have pulled a car close to the back door, wrapped the body in a sheet or a plastic tarp. Burned the tarp or stuck it in a dumpster. I've got guys looking. D.A.'s got guys looking. State police are looking."

"What about dental records?" Jamieson insisted.

"We have the remains. You get me some records to try a match with, and I'll get you the best damned forensic dentist you ever saw."

"These women," the INS man said angrily. "If they're illegal, they come here with nothing. No identification. No jobs. No family. No dental charts. No one to file a report when they don't show up."

"Probably," I said sweetly, "they don't expect to get killed. Inconsiderate of them."

Jamieson glared. I watched the pushpins on the map.

Mooney broke the silence. "Anyway, we're trying two dental matchups that aren't going to work. We're not doing them because of interagency pressure, we're doing them because we're thorough, got that? Very thorough.

"The thing I want to tell you is that the guy is going to be very hard to catch. Because he knows a lot of the same stuff cops know. Christ, he could *be* a cop. He's like that Atlanta child-murderer guy. He washes up afterward. He's careful. When we find him, he's going to have a library full of books on forensic medicine, stuff like that. Because this guy is not dumb and he's not ignorant, and he seems

145

to know what he's doing—if anybody who does this kind of shit knows what he's doing. You want to write that down?"

"I want the reports," Jamieson said stubbornly.

"Me too. How about you answer some questions? Why haven't I gotten a full set of prints to go with that green card? A set of documents? You gotta have prints, a medical report, a letter from a bank, from an employer, all that crap on file. At least I'd know if one of these stiffs is really named Manuela Estefan."

"I told you we're working on it."

Mooney got to his feet slowly. He's a big man, and when he stood, the tiny room got even smaller. For a minute I thought Jamieson was going to stand and challenge him, but he shrank back in his chair, and muttered, "First thing in the morning, then." He didn't say good-bye to me when he fled.

Mooney looked at me after a moment's silence. "Shit," he said, "I feel like the schoolyard bully."

"How long's he been here?" I asked.

"All day," Mooney said. "He wants to move in."

"Mooney," I said, "it'll be justifiable homicide. I'll testify."

"Take me out to dinner?" he said.

I was suddenly ravenous. "Sure, let's go," I said, thinking only of my stomach.

"You mean it?" I could tell from his eyes that he hadn't given up. Sam or no Sam. Gorgeous INS guys be damned.

"Yeah," I said less than graciously, "but it's not a date or anything."

"My treat," he said.

I wouldn't go till he agreed to split the bill.

We had three arguments before we left the station, which is about par for Mooney and me. First came the split-the-check controversy, followed closely by the where-to-eat routine, capped by the who-should-drive finale. I haven't figured out whether Mooney's insistence on driving is purely a macho thing or not. Could be he hates the way I drive, or it might be he thinks that if he drives, he'll get to take me home, wangle an invitation for a beer, and some night I'll extend the welcome up to my room. Who knows?

I had the advantage. My Toyota would get ticketed, towed, or stolen if I left it where it was, whereas Mooney's Buick was safe for all foreseeable eternity in the cop lot. I won.

We wholeheartedly agreed to eat at Mary Chung's in Central Square, each of us pretending the other had pulled a fast one and picked the restaurant. I can go without a hit of Mary's Suan La Chow Show for a week before I start getting withdrawal symptoms. It's a bowlful of plump wontons resting on beansprouts in a hot, spicy sauce that will cure whatever ails you. Sometimes I order two bowls. If the government declared it a restricted Class-A substance, I'd go outlaw.

I parked in the back lot after a fairly uneventful trip during which I exercised my horn only once. We made our way through a trash-strewn alleyway that seems narrower and smellier every year. A gang of young Haitians hangs out there, using it as a combination clubhouse and urinal. They grew quiet when we approached. Mooney doesn't look like a cop, but he looks like somebody you don't want to mess with. When I take the alley alone, they make comments. Usually that bothers the hell out of me, but it's harder to take offense at sexist slurs voiced in liquid French.

We had to wait twenty minutes for a booth, which is nothing. I wondered if M.I.T. was on vacation. Usually the place is clogged with Techies. You can tell from the decor that people come for the food.

Mooney does not eat Suan La Chow Show. It's too spicy for him. He ordered spring rolls. I've tried to educate him, but there it is.

We compromised on the rest of the order because I like everything spicy and Mooney likes everything bland —except he wouldn't call it bland, and he'd describe my taste as fiery. Lemon chicken, mostly for him; and hot stuffed eggplant, batter-fried and hot-pepper-sauced, mostly for me. The waitress left a pitcher of water on the table as well as a pot of tea.

"Just how much are you cooperating with Immigration on this investigation?" I asked. "Was that a sample?"

"A hundred and ten percent," Mooney answered disgustedly. "Word came down from on high. Do we have to talk about it?"

"You tell them everything," I murmured flatly, thinking about Marta's threat to leave town, taking Paolina away.

"Empty the whole bag," Mooney agreed. "Why?"

I poured steaming tea, dribbling it on the tabletop.

I wanted him to know about Hunneman's. I didn't want INS to rush in, raid it, and close it down.

"Is the cooperation a two-way street?" I asked when I'd fussed with the tea long enough for Mooney to start wondering whether I'd gone deaf. "I mean, why is it taking Jamieson so long to come up with the Manuela Estefan stuff?"

"Bureaucracy, pure and complex, far as I can tell. Other than the background on Estefan, they've got nothing."

"You know what kind of car Jamieson drives?"

"No." He took a tentative sip of his tea and set it down quickly. Too hot. "Why?"

I shrugged. "I don't like him."

"And usually you like everybody you meet on a case?"

"Sure," I said with a straight face. "You know me. Easy to get along with."

He opened his mouth, closed it, picked up his teacup, and tried again. He was grinning at me with his eyes.

The appetizers arrived, and we dug in like starving orphans. The wonton broth made my eyes water.

Mooney said, "Jamieson is the fastest paper-pusher I've ever met. He's filed so many goddamn interagency request forms, I could use a full-time liaison just to keep up with him. I don't have time for that crap, and I figure if he files the forms, he should at least have the decency to wait for us to file the responses instead of haunting my office. I don't like him much either. And now that the press has the story, they're breathing down my neck, yapping about how we should have called it a serial killing when we had the one body, or maybe before any corpses showed up, and the politicians want to get into the act and show how committed they are to the Hispanic community and—"

He stopped, shook his head like a wet dog, forked a bite of spring roll, and made a halfhearted stab at a grin. Then he said, "And how are you?"

I smiled ruefully, recognizing his attempt to turn the working motor off. "Okay. I don't think I've stopped running since seven this morning, and I can't remember the last time I sat down and ate a meal. Today lasted about two weeks."

"Yeah, tell me about it." He reached over and touched his fingertips to my cheek. "And tell me about this."

"Volleyball, Mooney. It's nothing."

"Boyfriend still out of the country and all?"

Boyfriend is such a quaint word. What Sam Gianelli is when he's in town is my lover. On again, off again, granted. But when it's on, we don't spend a lot of our time doing boyfriend-girlfriend things. Mooney probably has a quaint word for it. Premarital sex. Sin, maybe. Adultery. I'm divorced and Sam is, too, but Mooney's Catholic.

"Yeah," I said, resenting the sudden turn toward the personal when I hadn't even figured out a way to tell Mooney what I wanted to say. "You seeing anybody?"

"They hired a couple new uniforms who look promising," Mooney said.

I wondered how I'd feel seeing Mooney with somebody else. Maybe if I could get jealous, there'd be hope.

"Mooney," I said, "one thing you didn't mention when you were talking to Jamieson: the apartment. You find out anything about the apartment?"

"Huh?" Mooney said.

"The one on Westland."

"Back to business, huh?"

I inhaled a wonton, sneezed. Sometimes the sauce goes down the wrong way.

"You okay?"

150

"I was just wondering if you found out anything else about the place, Mooney."

"We talked to the landlord again," he said with a sigh. "You remember the skinny guy, name of Canfield. He's the one who manages the property, and he's probably pretty small potatoes. It's owned by a real-estate trust. Canfield, Oates, and Heffernan—and God knows how many silent partners. Tax-dodge shit. But can you hold somebody responsible because somebody got killed on their property? I could harass them if I wanted to, send out city-code violations and stuff. But Canfield says he didn't know more than one woman was living there, and he says he never even met her. I've posted a guy at the door, to be around if any of the other people who used to sleep on those beds shows up. Nobody has. And the room was pretty bare, no clothes except what you saw, no luggage."

"Maybe it was a staging area," I said. "A kind of safe house for illegals. One night's lodging while passing through."

"Could be. We don't know shit."

"I sent Roz over to the Cambridge Legal Collective to see if they've heard anything about the place."

"Good move," Mooney said. "Let me know."

It made me feel better to tell him something.

"Do you have any leads you're not talking about, Moon, any suspects?"

"Carlotta," he said patiently, "you know how this goes. No arrest within twenty-four hours and you can figure there's going to be no arrest for a while. Some of these killings are weeks old; one could be months. Every time the phone rings, I hope it's not another one, and then I think the only way we're going to nail the guy is if he tries

151

it again and screws up. And I'm afraid he won't screw up. You remember the profile of an FBI 'organized'?"

"Normal guy," I responded. "Drives a decent car. Married or has some kind of regular sex life, average or above-average intelligence . . ."

"And he's probably a first- or second-born child. Really helps yank him out of the general population."

All through dinner the urge to confess grew, filling my stomach till I barely did credit to the food. I gave him a play-by-play on the last volleyball game, detailing the circumstances of my injury and venting my feelings about Miss Boston College. I asked about his mom, but my heart wasn't in it. We gossiped about friends in the Department. Every time I'd weaken and get ready to spill it about Hunneman's, he'd mention Jamieson and I'd hold my tongue. Finally I made a deal with myself. I'd wait a day. One day. Until my business with the *Herald* lady was done, until it worked or failed.

There's a phone in Mary Chung's vestibule. I excused myself hurriedly, dialed Marta. I'd intended to call earlier, to make sure Paolina had come home safely, to see if mother and daughter had reconciled.

I let it ring twenty times. Then I called my answering machine, buzzed for messages. Paolina's clear, high voice sang over the line.

"I'm okay, Carlotta," she said carefully, "but I'm not going home. I just don't want to see my mother, not after what she said. Anyhow, don't worry. I'm safe and I'll call you soon. Bye."

The machine let out its dismal beep and started up again with a salesman's pitch for attractive aluminum siding for my home.

How had Paolina known I'd been at her apartment? Had she eavesdropped long enough to hear my voice? Had

Marta called me by name? Had she been hiding some-where? Had she watched me search for her under the stoop?

I was torn between relief that she'd called and fury that she hadn't told me where she was calling from, where this safe haven was.

I went back to the table. My fortune cookie was a bust, one of those good-things-come-to-nice-people lines. Mooney read his aloud: "You will have a romantic evening." But when I asked to see it, he wouldn't let me.

24

Mooney insisted on taking a cab home. Of course, I was expecting to drive him, either back to the station to fetch his car, or home, or wherever he wanted to go; otherwise I wouldn't have let him escort me through the smelly alleyway and walk me all the way to my car, only to backtrack and flag a cab on Mass. Ave. Mooney has a streak of gallantry that irritates me. It's not that I despise protective gestures; it's just that they infringe on my freedom. Maybe what I'm insisting on here is the right to get mugged at night in a bad neighborhood, but what the hell, it's my call.

I took Mass. Ave. to Harvard Square, executing the required bypass of its main intersection and U-turning my way back onto Brattle Street. I could have taken Huron Avenue, but Brattle's an attractive street to cruise. You get to pass by Henry Wadsworth Longfellow's house.

Lights blazed in my living-room window. I slipped the car into its spot in back of the house and hurried up the front walk, hoping to greet Paolina in the foyer.

I got the key in the lock and the door open before I heard the unexpected voice. It slowed my approach.

"Hello," said Harry Clinton.

"Hi," said Roz with an attempt to stifle a giggle.

They were seated too close together on the living-

155

room couch. Roz laughed awkwardly. Clinton stood and continued, "I hope you don't mind me waiting for you inside. Roz said you wouldn't."

He must have been there a while. Two empty glasses on the end table told the tale. Knowing Roz, I wondered if the encounter had progressed to intimacy. Most likely not; she had her clothes on, or at least she was wearing a subtle fuchsia T-shirt. Stretched tight across her chest, black letters said: AUNTIE EM, HATE YOU! HATE KANSAS! TAKING THE DOG. DOROTHY.

She got up and made a retreat toward the stairs, stammering meaningless, polite things like "Nice to have met you" and stuff. The T-shirt seemed to be all she had on, if you didn't count shoes. It was long enough for decency but not something I'd have recommended for answering the door to strangers. Her footsteps clattered up a flight. I listened to them fade.

"You keep weird office hours," I said briskly. "What can I do for you?"

"The bruising's not bad, and it doesn't look swollen."

My hand went automatically to my nose, touched my cheek.

"See a doctor?" he went on.

"No, Mom," I said.

"Okay, forget it. I hope you don't mind the late visit."

"Long as it's brief," I said.

"Blunt, aren't you?"

"Direct," I said. "I prefer direct."

He took two steps forward. He was tall, maybe three inches taller than me. He wore a white-and-blue plaid shirt tucked into jeans, both cut with a Western flair unobtainable in Harvard Square. "Well, then, directly," he said, "I came to tell you to lay off Hunneman's."

I swallowed air. "That's pretty blunt."

156

"It's an official Department request. If you don't back off, at least for a couple days, you're going to screw up a major undercover operation that's taken a hell of a lot of time and effort to set up. It's almost ripe, and the last thing we need is amateurs spooking the place."

I licked my lips and tasted Szechuan peppers, along with the residue of that hated word *amateur.* "Why the hell don't the cops know about this?" I asked. I never thought for a minute that Mooney might have kept it from me, which was dumb. If he had orders to shut up, he'd shut up.

"Key people know. No need to spread the word. We want to make sure the sleazeballs aren't warned—or alarmed by strange visitors."

Nobody had tailed me to Hunneman's. That meant an inside man, an undercover agent. Man or woman. I quickly reviewed the faces I'd seen at the factory.

"Who's this?" Clinton's drawl startled me. He'd moved across to the mantel, where he stood holding up a silver-framed photo of Paolina.

"My sister," I said.

"You don't look alike," he commented.

"She's my Little Sister from the Big Sisters organization."

"Nice," he said, setting the frame back carefully. "Pretty kid. She live close by?"

"Close," I said. "If she's home."

"Late to be out for a little girl."

"Yeah," I agreed. And I found myself telling Clinton about Paolina, how we'd met, how she'd changed, how worried I was about her. Chalk it up to anxiety, I guess. Told a perfect stranger something I hadn't told Mooney.

"She'll be fine," he said.

His easy assurance was sandpaper on my nerves.

157

"You don't have to worry about her," I snapped. "She's legal." I was tired as hell. Hints of my headache were coming back.

Clinton paced. "You don't like me, do you?"

"I don't like your job."

"You one of those people who think all cops are pigs? You think my job's easy? Or unnecessary? You think we should just pack up and go home and let anybody in the front door? Criminals and smugglers and people with contagious diseases?"

I flopped onto the couch. "My grandmother came over from Poland without a dime. I guess I'm for 'give me your tired, your poor.' That old stuff."

"Which worked fine when we had the whole goddamn frontier out there. When we had plenty of room for plenty of people. They were giving away land back then, for chrissake. Homesteading. You want a family of five homesteading on your property?"

"I'm tired," I said.

He went on as if he hadn't heard me. "And the hell of it is I almost agree with you. I work with a bunch of jerks. They've heard every hard-luck story so many times they don't hear anything anymore. They just file forms."

"Your buddy Jamieson's supposed to be a great one for that," I said. "He in on the Hunneman action?"

"Jamieson and I work together, but he's no buddy of mine. I'm not sure what he knows."

He came over and joined me on the couch, sitting a bit farther away than he had from Roz. Our thighs didn't touch. I found myself wondering what it would feel like if they did.

He said softly, "We got somebody tipping off illegal establishments before we can get it together for a raid. Somebody on the inside."

158

"You think Jamieson's the one?" Maybe that's why he was bird-dogging Mooney so closely, I thought. So he could warn somebody if the cops got hot.

"I didn't say that," Clinton insisted. "Jamieson's got a lot of years in the service and a lot of friends."

"Hard to believe the friends part."

"Yeah," he agreed with a grin, "I guess it is. Charming bastard, isn't he?" He stretched and stared around the room. "I like your place."

"I'm tired," I repeated. He'd given me a lot to mull over. I hoped I'd be able to sleep.

"Me too," he said, but he didn't take the hint and stand up to leave.

I hoped Roz hadn't invited him to spend the night with her. I was conscious again of his blue-jeaned thigh, a lot closer to mine than it had to be.

He said, "It's the little factories that employ the women these days. The men mostly work at the race-tracks, the stables. The pay's miserable and the bosses treat them like shit." He sighed deeply. "Somebody's got to stop it, you know. It's all very well to stand back and not get your hands dirty, but it doesn't do any good in the long run."

"I guess," I said reluctantly. I was only half hearing him, I was so damn sleepy.

And there he was, stretched out on my couch, relaxed, with his slow Southern drawl and easy grin, looking immovable and placid, like he'd just started the night. If he hadn't been so good-looking, I'd have kicked him out.

He picked up his glass off the table. "Can I bother you for a refill?"

"Of?"

"Roz and I split a Rolling Rock."

"One drink," I said. "Then I'm asleep."

"Okay, I appreciate it. Gets damn lonely out there. I guess I haven't made a lot of friends since I moved up here. Not like Jamieson."

"Feeling like an outsider?"

"Don't tell me I ain't, Yankee. The way I talk, the folks I work with think I oughta register with Immigration. They also think I'm practically retarded because my words don't come a thousand a minute."

I got the beer from the kitchen. As I walked toward the door I heard a scuffling noise on the stairway, probably T. C., who hadn't come out to greet me with his customary yowl. Maybe he was scared of Clinton. Jealous, more likely.

"Where you from?" I asked Clinton when I handed him his glass. He brushed my hand with his when he took it.

"Why, Texas, ma'am. Where else?"

"*¿Habla español?*"

"Like a native, ma'am."

"Why aren't you working out of Brownsville?"

"I got tired of chasing folks across the border. I got some family up here—"

"So much for the lonely-guy routine."

"Family ain't everything," he said. "I find these Yankee gals hard to get to know."

"Call 'em gals and you sure will," I said. "I could see how much trouble you were having with Roz. Real standoffish."

"She some kind of painter? She invited me up to see her acrylics."

"Not to be missed," I said dryly.

"Artists are strange," he said. "I've always been partial to volleyball players myself."

"You play?"

160

"Hoop's my game. Used to be, anyway. College stuff. I'm too old for college hoop—and college dating."

It reminded me of a blues lament: Too old for the orphanage, too young for the old-folks home. I grinned.

"You trying to say something?" I asked.

"Yeah," he said, "I am. See how fast you Yankees are? You married or anything?"

I hesitated for just a second too long. "I'm seeing somebody," I said.

"Permanent and exclusive, like?"

"He's out of town for a while."

"Far out of town?"

"Far," I agreed.

"Good," he said, "then maybe you'd have dinner with me Friday? I could make it Saturday too. In case you have to wash your hair Friday."

I smiled. "And what if I have to do my nails Saturday?"

"I don't know what you'd do to them, short and unpainted like they are."

"Saturday," I said, uttering a silent apology to Sam. He wasn't even sure when he'd be back. What the hell did he expect?

"I'll look forward to it."

"Me too."

"And remember the other stuff I said, not just my handsome face, okay?"

"When's the raid?" I asked.

"Soon. Unless something screws it up. Don't let it be you, okay?"

I nodded absently, yawned, and told him it was time to leave. I was half reluctant to see him go. As I let him out the door, he reached a hand over, tilted up my chin, kissed me gently on my bruised cheek. It was surprisingly

161

sweet. I turned and let him have my mouth, and we kissed for a while on the front porch like awkward teenagers on a first date.

He said, "I left one of my cards on the hall table. In case you threw the other one away."

I wondered if he'd kissed Roz.

I went inside and closed the door, leaning against the smooth wood. Then I bolted the door to keep me from rushing back out and inviting Clinton upstairs. His kisses, his hands, the strange musky smell of him left me breathing hard, made me realize how long Sam had been gone.

I dialed Marta's number. Paolina hadn't returned, and Marta was torn between worry and anger. I played her the tape. It didn't soothe her. She accused me of stealing her daughter, faking the tape, keeping Paolina hidden in my house. I warned her not to go to the factory. I'm not sure she heard me.

By the time I got her off the line, she'd awakened all my anxieties about Paolina. I'd been hoping to go to sleep with nothing but the memory of Harry Clinton's kisses on my lips. I was too tired even for that. As soon as I climbed in bed, the cool sheets surrounded me and dragged me down to sleep.

25

I slept until almost noon, which made me feel guilty because I missed Kristy's practice session. Usually I'm up early. Usually I don't cram my days as full. I scrunched under the covers and let faces roll through my memory like images on a loop of grainy film. Jamieson, Mooney, Hunneman, Lilia, Marta, the woman at the *Herald*. The *Herald* woman . . . I opened my eyes and checked the bedside clock. Plenty of time. I closed my eyes again. The faces that lingered were Paolina's and Clinton's.

And the woman who'd told me her name was Manuela Estefan.

I padded barefoot to the dresser and couldn't find the phone book. It's supposed to be near the phone, but it rarely is. Maybe Roz was painting its portrait somewhere. I dialed information and got the number of Paolina's school. I asked the woman who answered for the attendance officer, not really knowing if there was any such thing. But she connected me to another voice, and I asked if she could check on Paolina.

She could and did, and Paolina had not come to school. She wanted to ask me a few questions, but I hung up.

Showered and dressed, I went downstairs to scare up something to eat, checking for Clinton's card on the hall table along the way. It was gone. Good old Roz. I stood a long time in front of the refrigerator door before settling for cold cereal that was no more appetizing than it looked. I used the last of the milk, so I went to the fridge to add it to the shopping list.

I scrawled my addition and surveyed our message center on the refrigerator door. It was full of expired food coupons, take-out menus, and aged postcards. I decided I'd mention clearing the door to Roz. Then I saw it.

Hung on the tip of one of the magnets was a gold wire fish, Paolina's fish. I racked my memory for the last time she'd been at the house. When was the last time I'd really looked at the door? I couldn't remember, but I damned well would have spotted that fish.

Paolina had a key to the house. Paolina could have walked here from Marta's, a long walk. She could have taken the subway. I shook my head in rueful admiration. The kid was okay. She knew where to go to stay safe. It was like she'd said on the phone.

Relief turned to anger in seconds. I left the breakfast dishes on the table and ran up the stairs.

"Paolina!" I shouted. "I know you're here. Come on out."

I heard a noise in one of the bedrooms I used to rent to Harvard students, a place I now call my study, although I don't use it much. I called Paolina's name again, pushed the door ajar.

T. C., the cat, strolled out, head and tail held high and snooty. The room showed no other signs of habitation.

I remembered the scuffling cat noise I'd heard last night while getting that drink for Clinton. T. C. or Paolina?

I quickly searched the rest of the second floor, came to the conclusion that she must have stayed with Roz, and got angry all over again. A ten-year-old girl, out all night, and Roz keeps it a secret. Fuming at her irresponsibility, I trudged heavily up the steps.

I rapped sharply at the bedroom door, walked on in.

It looked like the house had been abandoned to me, the cat, and the bird. Nobody else around. An extra blanket lay on one of the tumbling mats. I touched the rough yellow wool and wished Paolina were still sheltered by its warmth. Not the strange, hostile child of the past few months but the little girl hiding somewhere in the tough new shell.

I hoped Roz had fed the girl breakfast. More likely Paolina had reminded Roz to eat.

I did a quick search of the room and found none of Paolina's clothes or books. I looked for strands of her hair and found two caught in Roz's hairbrush. They stood out against the garish blond ones, evidence enough for me.

I remembered Marta's harsh words on the phone last night, clattered downstairs to the nearest phone, and dialed her number.

A flood of Spanish and English gushed forth as soon as Marta realized who I was. I had trouble following it, but the gist seemed to be that Paolina had not come home, had not gone to school, and now she must call the police no matter what they did to her, and if they charged her with being an unfit mother, although why they should, she didn't know, where would her boys go and—

I broke in on the torrent, explained what I knew.

"You think I should call the police?" she asked.

"She'll probably come back here tonight. She doesn't know I know."

"Then we'll wait," Marta said grimly.

"Did you call Lilia?"

"Why?"

"Tell her to call in sick, okay?"

"You did it, didn't you? You went to the police."

"It's not me. It's something I heard. I think it would be better if Lilia stayed away for a while."

"I try to get hold of her."

"Thanks, Marta."

"You call me as soon as Paolina comes. I have things to say to her. Privately."

"I'll call."

I hung up and glanced at my watch. Time was getting short. I checked my clothes and changed out of my jeans. I put on khaki slacks, a jungle-print shirt, an olive-green sweater vest, and tucked my hair up under a slouch cap. We Boston cabbies have our dress code.

26

I kept my fingers crossed all the way over to Green & White. Gloria hadn't promised me a cab. Gloria rarely promises anything, but she almost always delivers.

She was on the phone when I walked into the office. Whenever I think about Gloria, a phone is part of the picture, as if one were permanently welded into the chink between her shoulder and neck. Food is also included.

She had a jumbo bag of Tootsie Rolls on her desk alongside an open jar of peanut butter. As I watched, she spoke into the receiver, peeled a Tootsie Roll, and plunged it into the peanut-butter jar. The candy came out with a massive scoop of yellowish goo on one end. Gloria stuck the whole mess in her mouth and kept on talking on the phone. I swear she didn't miss a syllable. I don't understand it, but I saw it. It made my teeth hurt.

Gloria should write a cookbook: *Junk Food Treats— Combinations Your Seven-year-old Never Thought Of.*

She hung up the phone and flashed me a smile, her teeth amazingly white.

"Got you a cab," she said. "When you gonna bring it back? Or shouldn't I ask?"

"Don't ask."

"Bring it back in one piece," she ordered. "You too."

167

Somebody once ran me off the road in a Green &
White. Gloria remembers.

"Listen," I said, "if Paolina calls or comes around,
give her a place to stay, okay? She's having trouble at
home."

"That's all you gonna tell me?"

"She ran away yesterday, stayed at my place last
night, except I didn't know it."

"And you a private eye and all," Gloria muttered. "I
always said that girl was sharp."

"Yeah," I said, "she is. And she may figure I'd catch on
if she spent more than one night. So if she comes to you,
call me, okay?"

"What if she don't want me to?"

"Gloria, she's not even eleven years old. Tell her what
you have to tell her, but let me know. The issue here is
safety, okay?"

"You telling me it's okay to lie to somebody long as
they're young enough?"

"Shit, Gloria," I said, taking down a key from the peg-
board, "I'm not trying to tell you anything. What a waste
of breath that would be."

"Those are the right keys," she called after me. "Have
a good ride. Any news from Sam?"

I pretended I hadn't heard her.

The car was one of Gloria's newer Fords, roomy
enough, with loose steering and rotten brakes. I flipped
off the two-way radio and turned on my tape deck, selecting an old Biograph blues collection. I turned the volume
up full-blast and squealed the tires on the way out of the
parking lot. I hoped Gloria heard me, but she was probably back on the phone, eating Tootsie Roll peanut-butter
glop.

I pulled off at a Dunkin' Donuts, bought half a dozen

assorted and two large coffees. From a phone booth I dialed the *Herald* advertising office and told Helen to go downstairs and wait for Cab Number 34, Green & White. She giggled, which I did not take as a heartening response.

I'd debated whether to seat her in the front or the rear. A cab with two in front looks odd. But a passenger idling at the taxi stand near the pillow factory would look a bit strange too. I waved her into the front seat. All Gloria's cabs have a plastic dividing shield that is supposed to stop bullets and effectively stops conversation.

"Didn't recognize you," she said. I sometimes think if I dyed my hair, my best friends wouldn't know who I was. You get so used to seeing that red that when I stick it up under a cap, the change is dramatic.

I recognized her. She still wore basic black, but this time it was skinny black jeans and a scoop-necked T-shirt of Day-Glo chartreuse, topped off with a black sweater that looked like moths had been chewing the elbows. She had chartreuse ribbons in her jet-black hair. This woman was obviously a conservative. Roz would have sprayed lines of chartreuse dye.

I turned down the music, softening a fine Robert Johnson riff.

"How'd you get the cab?" she asked. "Boost it?"

"Don't sweat," I said. "We won't get arrested."

"How long's this gonna take?"

"Depends how lucky we are. We're gonna park in a cab stand, and you'll look at some women and tell me if you see the one who brought that letter yesterday, and then I'll pay you. I don't want you identifying just anybody—"

"Hey, I wouldn't do that."

"Good. If you're not sure, say so. Anybody you think

169

of as a possible, I'll take her picture." I indicated the camera I'd placed on top of the meter.

"Hey, I could do that," she said. "I'm a great photographer."

And here I thought her only outlet for artistic expression was the candy-cane stripes on her fingernails.

"Well, I'd like to be a photographer," she amended, "but you can't make any good money at it." She hefted the camera. "You ought to have a tripod."

"I know. I thought it might be a little conspicuous."

She held the thirty-five-millimeter to her eye. "Good long lens on this thing," she said.

I'd borrowed it from Roz. She'd do the developing. For a price.

"I'd better take the shots," I said. "You concentrate on the faces."

I explained the layout to her on the way to Hunneman's. She asked very few questions, mainly about time and money, hers and mine.

I breathed a sigh of relief when I saw the cab stand was clear. I hadn't wanted to get into a chummy conversation with a Town Taxi driver or into any competition either. A one-cab stand in a bad part of town probably didn't bring in a day's wage. I wondered if anybody ever used it and hoped the INS hadn't picked it as a prime surveillance spot.

It was great for watching the bus stop. If the lady left in a car, it might be a bit more difficult. I yanked a pair of binoculars out of my handbag, and Helen spent some time focusing them. I told her to use them as little as possible, just on parking-lot ladies.

Hunneman's windowless storefront made staying unobserved easier, but I kept looking around for phone-company vans, delivery trucks, other possible INS vehicles. I didn't want Clinton to catch me ignoring his warning.

The cab got stuffy and I cranked down my window. I instructed Helen not to point, to describe the clothing of the women I should photograph. I warned her that they poured out the door fast. We ate doughnuts and drank coffee. She didn't demand much in the way of conversation, and I was grateful for that.

I warned her about the kerchiefs.

"I'll work on eyes and hair," she said.

"Think you can do it?"

"Photographer's eye," she boasted. "If she walks by, you just be ready to snap her."

Hunneman's doors yawned. I shrank back on the seat instinctively.

"Sit back," I barked at Helen. "The idea is to see them without getting seen."

"Whoa," she said. "There's a lot of 'em."

"Take them one at a time. Check out the ones who peel off to the parking lot first."

"Shit," Helen murmured. That was all she said for the next five minutes.

"Plaid skirt, pale blue blouse," Helen said. "Ten feet down the front walk."

"Sure?"

"Hell, no, she's just the closest I've seen."

She was walking toward the bus stop. I focused and shot through the front glass, hoping the glare wouldn't kill the image.

"Green blouse," Helen said. "She could be it. Got her?"

Another one heading for the bus stop. I hoped the bus would take its sweet time arriving. I picked up plaid skirt in another shot. Roz would have criticized the composition.

171

"This one with the beige flowered dress," Helen said.

"Well, which one is it?"

"I'm doing my damned best," she said.

I wondered if I should have brought more film. The third lady walked to a different bus stop, across the street. I saw Lilia out of the corner of my eye. Marta hadn't been able to stop her today.

"It's not the one getting into the gray Chevy on the lot, is it?" I asked.

"Nah."

Something to be grateful for.

The crowd started thinning. The bus on the far side of the street arrived.

"Which of the three is most likely?" I asked.

"Green blouse."

"Why?"

"I don't know. I'm not sure. The walk."

The bus swallowed up flowered dress. I could see another bus approaching in my rearview mirror. The women crowded toward the street, clutching their handbags.

"That's about it." Helen gave a deep, relieved sigh. "Doors have been closed a while."

The women streamed onto the bus.

"Take another look at those two," I said.

"Yeah," she said. "I think the green, but I'm not a hundred percent sure."

The bus took off. I hit the ignition and followed.

"Hey—" Helen said.

"I know, this isn't in the deal." I fumbled the agreed-upon cash out of my pocket, added ten more. "I'm going to drop you at the next light. Take a cab or something. If I need you, I'll be in touch."

She could follow orders. She put the binoculars down

on the seat and got her hand on the door handle, ready to fly. As soon as I stopped at the corner of North Beacon and Market, she was gone.

The bus turned left, and so did I.

27

As soon as I dumped Helen, I switched tapes and elevated the volume on my boom box. Rory Block came in loud and clear, singing about lovin' a country boy with hayseeds in his hair. My driving cap was starting to feel tight around the edges, so I ditched it, rearranging my hair with a shake of my head.

Buses are not a big challenge to tail. They're hard to lose, what with planned routes, behemoth size, and obliging city officials who paint numbers on each and every one. But following them has its drawbacks. This one, not one of the city's newer efforts, smelled. I kept dropping farther and farther back, but the odor remained overwhelming, and I had to breathe through my mouth.

The tricky part was checking out the bus stops. Not many folks departed at the first Market Street stops, which helped, and cabs can drive as erratically as they please in Boston, the benefit of a hard-won reputation. I've seen plenty weirder cab behavior than jerking to a stop twenty feet behind a bus. I mean, some desperate jockey might be hoping one of the heavily burdened women on the bus couldn't face the walk home.

I still hadn't decided whether to track Green Blouse or Plaid Skirt. Helen had declared Green Blouse her favorite, but she hadn't sounded too sure.

175

I wasn't familiar with the bus route. I thought a lot of different buses might plow down Market Street at some point or other, peeling off to Brighton Center, Cambridge Street, even Newton. I hoped the bus driver was one of those rare samaritans who believed in signaling.

The driver didn't believe in pulling fully into the right-hand lane to discharge passengers. I mean, why bother, when you can block the whole road? So screening the departing passengers wasn't as hard as it might have been. I recognized some of the Hunneman women by the kerchiefs around their necks. My two targets stayed on board.

In Brighton Center the bus flipped its left-turn signal and promptly pulled right to a dead stop. A blue Plymouth honked while its driver shoved a finger out the window. I caught a glimpse of Green Blouse climbing down the steps.

Quickly I slid over into the wake of the bus and shoved the cab into park. I was out on the street before I even thought about the legality of the maneuver.

Green Blouse was chatting with another woman at the bus stop, grinning and talking. I loitered, watching her reflection in a storefront window. Twenty-one would be about right, I thought. She had an unlined round face, mainly eyes and cheeks, with no discernible bone structure underneath. The green blouse was untidily tucked into a rust-colored skirt with a too-tight waistband. Either the skirt was borrowed or the woman had gained weight.

She said good-bye to her friend and started to walk away. I turned. Our eyes met.

She gasped, a sound audible more than thirty feet away, and fled, leaving her companion openmouthed. I had damn near the same reaction. I hadn't expected the woman to know me. I'd have tailed her a lot differently if I had.

I took off after her.

She hesitated a moment, then plunged into the open doors of a Woolworth's. I cursed. A big store full of aisles and crowds was all I needed. I pushed my way in past a nun buying a 3 Musketeers bar, gawked at the endless choices. Had Green Blouse gone for the plant aisle, the knitting and sewing area, the household goods? I took the center aisle, the path of least resistance, pushed all the way to the back of the store where the canaries and budgies fussed and whistled in their cages. At every crossroad I checked left and right. No Green Blouse.

I traveled the perimeter of the store next, counter-clockwise, looking down all the aisles. I saw a woman's shoe under a counter and approached it stealthily, frightening a store employee. I almost tripped over a rack of umbrellas.

I went back to the front door and paced there for fifteen long minutes, keeping track of all departing customers. Then I had the bright idea of asking whether there was another exit.

Just for the employees, the woman behind the counter said. I did another circuit and got what I expected. Nothing.

Damn. The woman must have known about the employees' exit, gone straight through.

Well, I'd taken her photograph. I could show it to Marta and get something to go on.

Sure. Marta had been damned cooperative so far.

I headed back to the cab. It had a line of angry cars behind it. Each one honked before giving up and pulling into the center lane. A silver-haired man in a three-piece suit leaned out his tinted BMW window and told me what the hell was wrong with the world and with people like me.

I couldn't have agreed with him more.

Roz was in the kitchen stoking her fires with peanut butter when I slammed the kitchen door by way of hostile greeting.

She didn't bother to turn. She held the refrigerator door open, using it for air-conditioning while she fingered peanut butter directly from jar to mouth. I got a good view of her butt, clad in skintight black leggings. I busied myself at the sink, which was laden with dirty dishes. I never do the dishes; that's Roz's job.

"You're gonna break those," she ventured finally when the clattering got too much for her nerves.

"Yeah," I muttered, "but at least they'll be clean."

"Leave it. I'll do 'em."

"This year?"

"Oooh, bad day, huh?"

"Yeah."

"Maybe I can—"

I turned to face her. She was out of the fridge by now, licking her index finger.

"You can try to explain about Paolina," I said. "But I doubt if you can. Shit, Roz, you let me spend the whole damn night wondering where she was, worrying—"

"She swore she'd run away if I told anyone. Anyone including you. I figured—"

179

"You should have figured out a way to tell me."

"I wanted her to trust me. She needed to trust somebody. She's all screwed up."

I shook water off some silverware, shoved it into a drawer without bothering to sort it, and banged the drawer shut.

"Well, where is she?" I demanded.

"I don't know," Roz said sheepishly, staring down at the floor. If she looked at the linoleum more often, I thought, she might get inspired to mop it.

"You're lying," I said. "She told you not to tell me."

"Honest, I don't have a clue," she maintained. "I'd tell you if I did."

"Like last night."

"You want to pick a fight, go ahead, but I don't know where she is."

"Do you know when she'll be back?"

"I don't even know if. She was gone when I got up."

"You didn't even feed her?"

"She was gone, Carlotta. Christ, what do you want me to say?"

"Shit." I dropped into a chair at the kitchen table.

"What's going on?" Roz asked.

"Good question." I ran my hand over the tabletop. It was gritty and sticky. Roz and I were overdue for a housework confrontation. I'm not fussy, but things were getting out of control. Maybe Roz was planning to do a series of acrylics featuring kitchen slime. "She overheard her mom say some nasty things about her. But there's something else. She's been cutting school a lot, ever since she got back from Colombia."

"Drugs?"

The minute you say Colombia, people think drugs. "Hell, no," I said. "She's ten years old."

180

"Since when did you get naïve?"

"Look, Roz, anything you can tell me—"

"Carlotta, I can't tell you about the kid. Not won't, can't. She didn't confide. I just figured better here than on the streets. That's all. But I can tell you something about the other business. That lawyer, the ritzy one from the Cambridge Legal Collective, called with the stuff you wanted, about the apartment building on Westland Avenue. Negative. She hasn't got any clients who claim to live there. Or on the whole block. And I read up on Hunneman Pillows. It's closely held, with stock owned in three names: mostly by a James Hunneman, but his wife has a chunk under the name Lydia Canfield, and then there's some under Blair Jeffries."

"Canfield," I repeated, drumming my fingers on the table.

"Yeah," she said, "sorry I didn't come up with anything else."

"If Paolina comes back, keep her here, for chrissake. I don't care if you tie her up."

"Where will you be?" Roz started to ask. But by then I had checked the phone book and was slamming the front door.

29

It was after six by the time I stuck my car in the lot behind the station. A fiery disk of sun crouched on the horizon, burning the western sky. The fading light brought an unexpected pang of regret. September and October are precious in New England, clear and crisp, painfully short. Between this Manuela business and the volleyball tournament I hadn't taken Paolina apple picking, or up to the White Mountains to view the sweep of changing foliage. The early sundown warned of coming winter.

I was relieved to find Mooney's Buick in the lot. He was in his office. As a bonus, he was alone.

I closed the door behind me.

He gazed up from a pile of papers. Tobacco smoke scented the air, and he held an unlit cigarette between the index and middle fingers of his right hand. He stared at it, placed it carefully in the top drawer of his desk, and closed the drawer.

"Can't make dinner tonight, Carlotta," he said with a forced grin. "All hell's breaking loose. Mayor wants task forces, I give him task forces. I got twenty extra bodies on this case all of a sudden. Nothing like a headline killing, especially in an election year."

"Yeah," I said.

He tapped his finger on a pile of yellowed folders.

183

"Foley's pulling jackets on all known sex offenders. We're checking parolees from Bridgewater. There's been a string of violent robberies in the Fens and we're squeezing snitches to see if these killings could be related. Your friend Triola's doing traffic tickets for the areas where the corpses were found. That turned the trick for the Son of Sam guys."

"Busy," I said.

"You bet. Some of it's out of headquarters. Some at D. Some state. District attorney's giving us full cooperation." He blew out a deep breath and flexed his shoulders. "All ticking away, going like clockwork—and I start smoking again."

I sat in the chair across from him. "Mooney, who owns the place on Westland? Run that by me again."

"A whole month with no butts, and today I had to light up."

"It's tough," I said. I quit three years ago. I could probably give you month, day, and time.

He emptied his ashtray into the wastebasket under his desk, as if hiding the evidence could revoke the act. "Makes me feel like a jerk. Glad I don't work narcotics. How can you run around busting people for drugs while you're sucking on a butt?"

"A lot of cops do, Mooney, and they don't even think about it. About Westland Avenue, there was a guy named Canfield involved, right?"

"Three guys fronting for a real-estate trust. Canfield, Oates, and Heffernan. Canfield's the landlord, the only up-front one. There could be a whole slew of secret partners we don't know shit about. Why?"

"If your Canfield's connected to my Canfield, I may have something."

"Two Canfields, Carlotta? It's a fairly common name."

184

"Just nine in the phone book, Mooney. Humor me."

"Humor's something I'm low on. Set me straight. Are you trying to make a neat little package out of a string of random deaths? I got fifteen guys trying to get some connection between the victims, and a fat lot of good it did 'em down in New Bedford. They know most of those women hung around the same bars, used drugs—"

"Mooney—" I tried to interrupt but he had more to say.

"Serial killings make sense, Carlotta. But it's a kind of sense only lunatics understand. They act out some fantasy or relive some dream sequence or some memory from a screwy childhood. I make this guy as Hispanic, because his fantasy revolves around Hispanic women. Maybe his mother, maybe his wife, maybe somebody he dated or wanted to date—"

"Mooney, I've got something that connects the name Manuela Estefan to a place where a lot of illegals work. And there could be a connection to Westland Avenue, if your Canfield knows my Canfield."

He pushed aside his folders, took the cigarette out of his desk drawer, and lit it with an air halfway between defeat and defiance. "My Canfield is Harold. Harold J."

"Mine is a woman. Lydia. She's part owner of the place."

"Married to Harold?"

"Won't work. Mine's married to a James Hunneman." I waited to see if the name Hunneman registered.

"How'd you make this connection?"

"Tip," I said.

"Go on. I don't want to have to pry this out of you."

"You might already know about it from INS," I said cautiously.

Mooney inhaled tobacco as if he were drawing energy from it. "Jamieson hasn't been sharing."

"They're planning a raid at the Hunneman Pillow Factory. In Brighton. They've got somebody undercover."

"Wait a fucking minute. You saying they know there's a connection to a homicide and they're sitting on it?"

"I'm not sure what they know."

"Who's they?"

"I heard it from a colleague of Jamieson's, guy named Clinton."

"I haven't even been able to reach that Jamieson jerk today. Some secretary keeps telling me he's unavailable. Want to know why? Because he hasn't given me a scrap of backup on that Manuela Estefan green card."

"That doesn't make sense."

"Bingo. He left me a long, detailed bullshit message about some bureaucratic screwup, but I'm not sure I buy it."

I yanked at a strand of my hair and wondered when I'd stop wanting a smoke. "It's not a counterfeit card, right?" I said slowly. "But it's not a documented card either."

Mooney's mouth spread into a smug grin, and I knew we were thinking along similar lines. "Sound familiar?" he asked. "Ring any bells?"

"The fake drivers' licenses," I murmured, referring to a local scandal that had been brewing for the past three months.

"And those were issued by a regular clerk at the Registry of Motor Vehicles," Mooney agreed. "Legit licenses, no forgery involved. So maybe I can't get hold of Jamieson because somebody at INS is peddling 'genuine' green cards for a fee. Maybe he doesn't want to air dirty INS linen in front of the Boston cops." Mooney lit another cigarette from the butt of the one he'd just smoked. "The thing I can't figure is whether this has anything to do with the killings or if it's just a sidebar."

I started unburdening my soul, telling him everything I knew about the pillow factory with the emphasis slightly bent so it wouldn't look like I'd been keeping secrets. I'd barely begun when somebody knocked on the door and flung it open at the same moment.

"Dave," Mooney said to a narrow-faced man in a leather jacket, "I'm busy here. Can it keep?"

"Guess so," the cop answered, shrugging his shoulders. "We picked her up in front of the Westland place. Kind of loitering. I questioned her, sort of, and I don't think she knows much. Says she's looking for a place to live and somebody gave her that address, or she read it in the paper, or she saw it on a sign on a tree. She doesn't remember. Or she doesn't understand English. Cooperative. I don't really know what we can hold her on, but I thought—"

By that time I'd swiveled in my chair. The cop was holding her above the elbow, not gently, but not so tight as to cause any bruises.

"Jesus Christ, Mooney," I said. "Jackpot. Bring her in."

Green Blouse stared at me. She muttered something under her breath in Spanish and made the sign of the cross on her chest. Then she started to cry.

30

"I didn't realize you had that effect on women," Mooney said, raising an eyebrow in my direction.

"Shut up," I responded automatically. Then I turned to Green Blouse and murmured, "It's okay, come on, sit down." To the gawking cop who'd brought her, I said, "Get her some Kleenex or something, for chrissake." I turned back to the woman and muttered in halting Spanish that everything was going to be all right.

She cried harder. Close up, she looked even younger, her matronly clothes and plump body lending her a maturity her smooth circle of a face denied. I patted her shoulder awkwardly. Someone slammed a Kleenex box down on Mooney's desk. I thrust a wad of tissues into the girl's hand. She dammed her eyes with them and subsided into snuffles and gulps.

"They won't hurt you," I said. Mooney gave me a sharp glance on the *they*. He caught on quickly. I was on her side, protecting her from the police. It was going to be the two of us against the big bad men. Hell, it might work.

Her hand closed on mine with a surprisingly firm grip. *"No salga,"* she pleaded, staring at me from under long lashes. Don't leave.

"I'm not going anywhere," I said, as much for Mooney's benefit as for hers. I wasn't sure she understood anything I said in English. "I think we ought to get a translator in here."

"A lawyer?"

I shrugged. "If the conversation seems to point that way, we can back off and get one."

"Dave," Mooney barked, "Mendez at his desk?"

"Is there a woman?" I asked. Mooney gave me the eye and I said, "Well, I just thought she'd be more comfortable."

"Check," Mooney ordered tersely, and the cop named Dave disappeared.

"How do you know her?" Mooney spoke as soon as the door closed. He'd been dying to ask but hadn't wanted to in front of Dave. The lieutenant's always supposed to know what's going on. I grinned at him to show I knew his tricks as well as he knew mine.

"This is my tipster. At least I think she is. She ran like a scared rabbit when I tried to find out. You must have gone to Westland Avenue right after you got away from me in Woolworth's." I addressed the last sentence to the woman. I might as well have saved my breath. Her eyes darted around the small room as if she were searching for a secret exit.

A thin cop with a wispy mustache followed Dave through the door. Five was a crowd for Mooney's office, but I didn't think a switch to an interrogation room would improve things. The mustached cop shot off a quick Spanish volley at our guest, shook her hand formally, nodded at each of us as he made introductions. I could follow him pretty well. I don't think Mooney caught more than his own name.

"Her name is Ana Uribe Palma. She's scared," the cop said.

Why not, I thought.

Then Mooney announced, "Since Ms. Carlyle already knows Señorita Uribe, she'll start things off." Mooney's a master at stuff like that. I mean, look at that one sentence. Dumps the work on me and at the same time lets the other guys know he's in charge.

There were so many questions I wanted to ask that for a moment my mind went blank. I decided to start at ground zero.

"Señorita Uribe—*¿La puedo llama Ana?*" May I call you Ana?

"*Sí.*"

"Ana," I said gently, "*¿Quién es Manuela Estefan?*" Who is Manuela Estefan?

She must have expected it, but the name startled her all the same. Her eyes made the circuit of the tiny room again, came up with the same answer: no way out.

"*Una mujer,*" she answered cautiously. "A woman like me works at the factory."

Mooney sat up straighter. Someone who actually knew Manuela Estefan.

I said, "You could find her for us at the factory. Point her out to us." I spoke English now and waited for Mendez to translate. I didn't want to make a mistake.

"No. No, she no work there anymore."

"Where did she go?"

"*No sé.*" I don't know. Her chin quivered and tears formed standing pools in her eyes.

"Mooney, do you have Manuela's green card?" I asked, signaling to Mendez not to translate the aside.

"Yeah."

"Give it to me."

I asked Mooney if I could remove it from the evidence bag and he nodded. I passed it over to Ana, and she took it

191

solemnly, stared at it, and pressed it to her breast. The tears welled up and started to fall.

"Please, have you seen her?" she asked eagerly.

"Is this a picture of Manuela?" I asked.

"Sí."

"Was Manuela your friend?"

"Sí." Oh, yes. Manuela was her good friend.

Her cheerful burst of words made my throat dry. "Ana, I'm sorry to tell you this, but I believe the woman who had this card is dead. No one can hurt her. Nothing you tell me can hurt her anymore." Manuela Estefan had to be one of the dead women. Why cut off the hands unless the killer was afraid of identification? What identification did we have except the lone green card?

"No," Ana said, her dark eyes narrowing with suspicion, "you try to trick me."

"No tricks."

"I no betray my friend," she insisted, gulping, glancing from Mooney to Dave as if she expected them to haul out the rubber hoses.

I said, "Listen to me. If Manuela was your friend, you betray her with your silence. Please, for her sake and yours, talk about her. Talk about the women at the factory, the apartment on Westland, the—"

"You know, then."

"Some I know."

She murmured, "Manuela, she is the strong one, the one who decides, the one who speaks well and acts brave. I must go to church and light a candle for her."

I thought she might start to weep again, so I slipped another question in quickly. "How long since you've seen Manuela?"

"Many months. With her green card she is like a North American. She can work anywhere, go anywhere—

192

to California, even, where it is always warm like home. She is a free woman, like you."

"How did Manuela get her green card?"

"You say she is dead, not in jail, not in El Salvador? I would not tell you if—"

"She's dead." God forgive me if I'm wrong, I thought.

Ana hung her head. "Then I, too, am dead."

"Ana." I took her hand and squeezed her plump fingers. "Help us and we can make you safe."

For a minute I thought she would spill everything. Her eyes wavered. She stared at the green card as if the image of Manuela Estefan could speak to her. "But I know nothing," she said finally, her voice close to a moan. She avoided my eyes, ducking her head and staring at the desktop.

"Tell me about the apartment, about the factory," I insisted, keeping my voice low and even.

"There is nothing to tell. *Nada.* I live at the apartment with other women. We work at the factory."

"What women? What are their names? Can we talk to them?"

The tears started to fall again. "They are gone. They go away. The women at the factory, when they get their papers, they go away."

"Where?"

"I don't know. The boss at the factory says they get papers, they get green cards, they go."

"What's the name of this factory?" Dave asked. Mooney frowned at him.

"Go on, Ana," I prompted.

"Maybe they all go to California. We talk about California. Maybe they get jobs selling pretty dresses at fine stores, or better, selling clothes to rich men who look for girls to marry."

193

Mendez repeated everything. His words became a regular echo, background noise. His droning voice hardly interrupted the flow.

Ana's fantasies sounded singsong-rehearsed, as if she'd repeated them to herself a thousand times. While she spoke, she stared at Manuela's green card, grasping it so tightly that her thumb and forefingers whitened.

"Why did you leave the message at the newspaper office?" I asked.

"Someone reads me the words from the newspaper. I think maybe Manuela tries to reach me, or one of the others—I think after so long there is no harm in it, but then I am frightened."

"But you recognized me."

She stared at the card for inspiration. "No, *señorita,*" she said dully. "You are mistaken. Please, what will they do with me now? *¿La policía?* I have no papers."

I ignored her query. "But you did work with Manuela Estefan, and you lived at Westland Avenue—also with Manuela?"

"*Sí.*"

"And how many others?"

"Maybe three other women."

"And why did you leave Westland Avenue?"

"The boss says *La Migra* knows about the apartment. We must go."

"You packed up your clothes?"

"No, one of the men from the factory goes and does that while we work. It happens too fast."

"Which man?"

"I don't know."

"And why did you decide to go back to the apartment today?"

She consulted the image of Manuela. "I, uh, I think maybe I leave something there."

Sure. Something that was worth taking a risk with *La Migra*. Whatever she saw in the depths of that green card was telling her to lie.

"Do you drive a car?"

"I have no license, *señorita.*"

"How long have you been in this country?"

"Four months only."

"Did Manuela bring you here? Was she your coyote, your guide?"

She seemed puzzled by my question. "No, *señorita.*"

"How did you get here, how did you come to Boston?"

"I walk many miles. I take the bus."

"Who helped you?"

"I walk and take the bus. That is all."

I breathed in and out, staring at Mooney. I realized who Ana was starting to remind me of. Marta. Marta in one of her stubborn moods. I changed direction, hoping to surprise the woman into a truthful response. "What are the names of the women who lived with you at the apartment?"

She hesitated. "Manuela you know. The others are Aurelia—"

"Aurelia Gaitan?" Mooney interrupted.

"Yes, I think. And then there is Delores and Amalia and me."

"Last names? Family names?"

"*No sé.* Please, *señorita,* what will happen to me?"

Dave said, "Maybe she can clear up the IDs on the stiffs."

Mooney glanced at him sharply. He seemed to be remembering what the dead women looked like with their butchered hands and mauled faces. He said, "First we'll

195

have her look at their personal effects. See if you can get them up here."

I wondered if Ana, quietly sobbing at the table, would identify the silver filigree ring as belonging to Manuela or Aurelia or Delores or Amalia.

The words of an old Woody Guthrie song came unbidden to my mind. He wrote it in the fifties after a plane crash in California, over Los Gatos Canyon.

> Good-bye to my Juan, good-bye Rosalita,
> Adiós, mis amigos, Jesús y María,
> You won't have a name when you ride the big airplane,
> All they will call you will be deportees.

When the plane crashed and everyone died, nobody knew who the passengers were. Nobody knew how many died. They were just illegal aliens, just deportees.

31

Dave made a brief phone call and took off for the property room downstairs.

Mooney murmured, "Think we can talk in front of her?"

I shook my head no. I wasn't sure how much English Ana understood. My buddy Marta certainly caught a lot more than she let on. Ana's eyes were the same deep brown. They gave little away. Mooney nodded me out the door after telling Mendez to stay put.

"Please, *señorita. No salga, por favor. No salga.*"

I assured her I'd be right back. She clutched at my hand and regarded the slightly built Mendez with suspicion. Why she wanted me to stay and listen to her evasions, I wasn't sure. She didn't trust me.

"She's lying," I said as soon as we'd put some distance between us and the closed office door.

"Well, of course she's lying," Mooney growled, leaning against the coffee machine. "She's scared. She didn't choose to come in here and dump the bag. The question is *how* she's lying. Is what she says a lie, or is the lie in what she isn't saying?"

"She's leaving stuff out. There's a link between the dead women and Westland Avenue. We knew that. And

197

now we know there's another link, to this Hunneman Pillow Factory."

Mooney ran a hand over his jaw as if he were checking to see when he'd last shaved. "At least I can call off the decoys at the bus station. I've got every Hispanic woman on the force playing hooker down in Park Square, trying to lure some random psycho. Our psycho has to have a connection to one of those two places, preferably both."

"*If* she identifies the effects—or the bodies."

"Yeah. If. What was that stuff about coyotes, about the Estefan woman bringing in illegals? Where'd you get that?"

"INS. They thought she might have been killed by someone who didn't like her line of work."

"Hell, your guy's freer with his theories than mine is. I've got to get everybody associated with that factory in here for questioning."

Dave and a uniform appeared, each holding two large brown-paper bags. I turned to go back into the office.

Mooney stopped me with a hand on my shoulder. "You ever find out why that woman came to you? Back at the beginning? The dead woman?"

I couldn't keep her out of it any longer. "Paolina's mother works at the factory every once in a while. She didn't want to tell me about it, afraid Welfare will cut her benefits if they find out she works."

"I'll need to talk to her."

"Oh, Mooney, you know how she is with cops. I'll get more out of her in her kitchen than you'll ever get from her down here."

"I want a list of every man she's ever seen at the factory. Full descriptions. Names."

"Everything," I promised. I didn't tell him I'd already tried.

Dave and Mendez cleared Mooney's desk and set down the brown-paper bags. The property officer departed. Ana, scrunched down small in her chair, seemed relieved to see me.

The bags were stapled shut. Each was fastened with a manila tag looped to a string closure. You had to sign the tags if you authorized examination of the contents. Mooney signed. Dave started removing staples, and I joined in. Dave had a gadget designed for the task. I used a scissors blade and managed to cut myself. I couldn't remember when I'd last had a tetanus shot.

"Should we take the stuff out or let her do it?" I asked. I was whispering. I don't know why. Ana was staring apprehensively at the bags. I reached over and touched her shoulder.

The bags smelled musty.

Mooney told Mendez to help Ana unload the bags and to keep track of exactly what she said, translating every word. He told Dave to take notes.

For a while there was only the noise of crinkling paper, rustling cloth.

Mooney looked away, addressed me. "This 'boss,' the factory owner, could be the key. He must know something's going on, even if he isn't the crazy."

I recalled my brief encounter with James Hunneman. He'd reminded me of a schoolyard bully, with his florid face and arrogant manner. But a killer?

I couldn't keep my eyes off Ana. She didn't want to look in the bags. Mendez was taking it slowly, explaining that it was only clothing and maybe she could help us if she saw something familiar. Nothing to be afraid of.

"Carlotta," Mooney said.

"Canfield," I said. "The landlord at Westland Avenue.

It would be nice if he had a connection to the pillow factory."

"Yeah. We can bring him in and talk it over. It'll take time. Guys who own apartments have money and lawyers."

Ana said something that Mendez didn't get. He couldn't have, it came out so garbled. She was holding a stained blouse in her hand, staring at the sleeve, at a tiny bit of embroidery, running her fingers over it.

"Think Ana's in danger?" Mooney asked.

"If the killer has any idea she's talking to the cops, I wouldn't take out insurance on her," I said.

"La blusa." Ana finally said something clearly enough for me to understand.

"What about the blouse?" Mendez murmured.

"Es de Manuela," she said faintly. "I stitch it for her. I sew better than her. It is one thing I do better." Her shoulders shook. She raised her left hand to her mouth; it rubbed her lips, her cheek, her forehead, before coming to rest across her eyes, blocking her vision. Dave ignored her, writing down only what Mendez said, looking only at Mendez. It was painful to look at Ana. I couldn't tear my eyes away.

"Lo siento," I murmured. I'm sorry. She lowered her hand and looked at me with such agony, that I wished I'd kept still.

"Is she going to have to stay here, Mooney?"

"I'd say yes, for her own good."

"Maybe protective custody is the way to go," I said slowly. "I'll call a lawyer. If Ana helps you nab this guy, I think there ought to be some quid pro quo stuff with INS —and I don't want her staying in a cell."

"We can put her in a hotel room with a policewoman."

200

"Joanne?"

"Maybe."

Jo Triola's a good friend of mine on the force. And she speaks Spanish.

"Who you gonna call for a lawyer?" Mooney asked. "PD?"

"One of the attorneys over at the Cambridge Legal Collective, Marian Rutledge."

"Okay."

The room seemed unnaturally quiet. Ana's crying had given way to silence punctuated by hiccuping gulps. She fingered the tattered clothing, the worn shoes. Every once in a while she would moan, *"Jesús, María,"* close her eyes, and turn away. And Mendez would gently lead her back to yet another bag, another dead friend.

The smell of decay had entered the room, and I wished the city had been kind enough to give Mooney an office with a window.

"Tell me again about the INS," Mooney said. I'm sure he got it the first time. He just wanted to have something to do besides stare at Ana's grief. I was glad he asked. The room seemed to be getting warmer. I was starting to sweat.

"All I know is that they've got Hunneman's under surveillance—for immigration violations, I guess. They've got plenty of violations. And I think there's an undercover guy in there, somebody who works for INS."

"Don't they know about the killer? Are they dumb enough to try to nab him without bringing in the cops? That's our fucking job."

"Mooney, all I know is the guy who told me didn't seem to trust anybody, especially not Jamieson. He thought somebody at INS was on the take, that they'd

201

warn Hunneman and screw the raid. And Marta thinks cops are taking bribes."

"Turncoats everywhere, huh?"

"Or paranoia."

"I used to know a decent Joe at INS—somebody I'd be willing to trust on this."

"Good," I said. "Get in touch with him."

"And I'm gonna have this Canfield brought in. Long night ahead."

Not as long as Ana's, I thought. Not as lonely.

"How can you tell if it's day or night in here?" I asked. "I'm going to head over to Marta's."

"Okay," he said.

Ana unfolded the last bag, reached in, and drew out the silver filigree ring. She made a noise like a small animal, a noise wrenched from deep within her.

Manuela, I thought. Amalia, Delores, Aurelia. Somehow their names seemed very important to me.

"Mooney, one thing you might look for when you get some bodies in for questioning: Find out if anybody drives a white Aries."

"Why?"

I told him about the car that had followed me. He digested the tale in silence.

"Before you go, Carlotta, ask Ana if she has any more to tell us. Maybe she'll believe us now."

I tried. I did my best. I held her hand while Mendez murmured soothing lies about how everything was going to turn out all right in the end. But her distrust, or maybe her fear, was too strong.

I rapped on the door of Marta's building, hollered her name while inwardly cursing the lazy creep of a superintendent who hadn't fixed the buzzer yet. I was hoping that Paolina would hurry down the stairs to let me in.

Instead I heard Marta's heavy tread, her cane punctuating the difficult descent.

She'd been hoping for Paolina too. The angry sparkle went out of her eyes when she saw me, leaving them wary and cool. We faced each other, both too tired to hide our mutual disappointment.

"She's with you?" Marta demanded.

"No."

"She's at your house?"

"She was there last night. I told you. She may come back. Right now it's you I need to talk to."

"Talk," she repeated bleakly, shaking her head. But she held the door wide.

The apartment was immaculate, sofa bed returned to its sofa disguise, pillows neatly plumped. Floors vacuumed, end tables shined. Marta must have found waiting intolerable, even cleaning preferable. Kept the mind occupied, kept the body moving, kept you from hearing the tick of the clock, the dead silence of the unringing phone.

The living room looked like a stage set.

Marta said, "Lilia has the boys. I thought when she comes home, the two of us should be alone."

For once the TV screen was blank. Marta waved me into the tiny kitchen. The table was covered with oddly shaped packages wrapped in aluminum foil and waxed paper. The door to the freezer compartment of the ancient GE refrigerator hung open. A kettle steamed on the stove.

"What do you want?" Marta said, selecting a blunt knife from a jumbled drawerful. "Why don't you find her? Why doesn't she come home? What was so bad here for her?"

I couldn't answer all the questions, and I knew better than to try. I stuck to the first one. "I need to know more about the Hunneman plant."

She stared at me with angry eyes, hefted the knife in her hand. "Please," she said, "all I think about is my daughter."

"I know," I said.

"You don't know anything," she replied bitterly. She poured boiling water into a shallow tray, set it with a bang on the ice-caked bottom shelf of the freezer.

"I know this has to be done," I said, "either here or at the police station. Tonight."

"The police!" She smacked her palm against the refrigerator door. "You tell the police. *Jesús y María*, I tell you before, they close it down. You got no sense."

"Women who work there die, Marta. Four women are dead. You could be in danger. Lilia could be in danger."

She gripped the handle of the blunt knife. "I don't know nothing," she said angrily, turning away and stabbing viciously at the ice-coated walls of the freezer.

"Then let's go over to Lilia's. I'll talk to her."

"I can't leave here in the middle of this. What if Paolina comes? I won't go." A hunk of grayish ice fell and clattered across the linoleum.

I picked it up and chucked it in the sink. "Then tell me what you know."

"You tell the police about me?"

"Just one man. A friend. I'll try to keep you out of it. You know that."

She kept chipping at the ice. "I know if I go to jail, maybe you think you have my daughter for your own."

I sat on a hard wooden chair. I felt like Marta had peeled back a layer of my skin, exposed something I hadn't even acknowledged to myself. I haven't thought about kids since Cal and I split up. Was that because I was fooling myself about Paolina? Not about the way I felt for her but about the way she felt for me.

Marta didn't press her advantage. Water was starting to leak down the side of the freezer and puddle on the floor. "At the factory," she said, "I do my work. I keep my head down. I don't look at things and people that don't concern me."

"Marta," I said impatiently, "this is serious. You talk to me or you talk to the police."

She kept on defrosting the freezer, chipping and hacking at the dirty ice, but she answered my questions. The man she saw the most was the beer-bellied security guard I'd encountered on my brief foray into the plant. There were two shift supervisors, the "boss," who was spoken of and never seen, and another security guard, who might have been Hispanic.

She swabbed the inside of the freezer with a rag. "I'm only there a few days. I don't know so much. Maybe Lilia knows. But if Lilia helps, she'll be in trouble, with no papers—"

"I'll make sure she has a lawyer—"

"A lawyer. A thief, more like it." Marta rummaged through the frozen parcels. She dropped one with a thud and I remembered old Mr. Binkleman who lived in the apartment below. "It's Paolina who makes all this trouble for us."

"Come on, Marta. You can't blame her for everything."

"For this, yes! It's Paolina who talks to that woman about you, gives her your business card. Showing off, that's what she's doing. It's not me who talks. I know better than to shoot off my mouth."

It seemed as if the temperature had suddenly dropped ten degrees. As if the freezer had taken charge, ice-coating the room. I could hear the clock tick. "What was Paolina doing there?" I said quietly. It took effort not to scream, not to grab Marta and shake her by her shoulders till her foolish head snapped against the refrigerator door.

Marta repacked the freezer compartment as she spoke, angrily chucking packaged waffles next to frozen pizzas. "She won't go to school. How can I leave her here, a place like this? In the daytime the boys downstairs, they have the drugs, wine, whatever. The words you hear are obscene, the noises obscene. I cannot leave her here. I need to work so she comes along. She learns like in a school. She learns to work, a better thing than what she learns in school. Learn to make money, I tell her."

If it got any colder, my teeth would start to chatter.

"What is it?" Marta asked. "You okay?"

I stood abruptly. "If Paolina comes home, you call me. No matter what time of night it is, no matter if it's two in the morning, you call me. Understand?"

"You got no business talking to me like that, yelling at me, just because my crazy daughter runs away."

With an effort I calmed my voice. "Marta, if you know why she ran away, tell me. Please."

She studied a package of frozen piecrust. "You think this is still good?" she muttered. "I can't find no date on it."

"Is your husband back in town?" I asked. "Is that what's bothering Paolina?"

Marta shoved the questionable piecrust to the back of the freezer, pivoted to face me. "Pedro? He wouldn't come back here. What makes you think Pedro's here?"

"You were comparing him to Paolina when she ran off, remember?" In very unkind terms, but I didn't say that.

Marta sank heavily into a kitchen chair. She opened and closed her right hand, staring at the swollen knuckles. The pain made her wince. "You don't understand," she said.

"Paolina said the same thing to me."

Marta made a show of sorting through the remaining frozen foods, inspecting masking-tape labels. She avoided my eyes. "It wasn't Pedro I was yelling about. Pedro is not Paolina's father."

I ran my tongue over my lips. "He's not—"

"You want to listen to me or you want to talk? Paolina's father, he's a rich man. But does that help us here, living like pigs? Do we get anything? No. Her grandfather dies in Colombia, leaves a fortune, a million dollars, more, and what do we get? A little money for a new television. That's all."

"Wait a minute," I said, holding up my hand to stop her angry words. "Does Paolina know?"

"She knows nothing. She's too young. This rich Colombian man, I'm working in his house, a little cleaning, a little cooking. He says he's going to marry me, but when

207

I'm pregnant with Paolina, then it's good-bye, he's got too many important things to do, with the M-19, the *guerrillas*, the Communists. A man with ideas, he tells me, can't be chained to a woman like me, a woman with a child; a woman can't live on the run from the government."

Her hair had come loose from its tight bun. As she spoke, she unpinned it. It fell, heavy and lank, to her shoulders. She rubbed her temples, closed her eyes. For a moment I got a glimpse of the young woman she must have been, with a fresh, unlined face, a face like Paolina's.

"He gives me a little money to ease his conscience, and I come to this country after I have my child, my Paolina. I meet Pedro when she is just a baby. He says he loves us both." She sighed deeply, shrugged her shoulders. "Maybe he did, for a while."

"How could you keep this a secret? How could you not tell her?"

"What difference does it make?" she said. "What difference would it make? It's an old story. It happened a long time ago."

"But how can you be sure Paolina doesn't know? If you went to see her grandfather—"

"I wouldn't go, not to beg for money, not if I'm healthy, not if I can work. Paolina knows nothing. She's just a child," Marta insisted. "She doesn't understand. I talk to the old man at night. I bring her with me, yes. To show the old man she looks like her father. But she's sleepy. She visits with the housemaid. She falls asleep."

I thought about Paolina's behavior since she'd returned from Colombia. "She knows," I said. "Maybe not everything, but something."

"So what?" Marta said, defiantly sticking her hairpins

208

back where they belonged. "So she accepts what is. What else can she do?"

"I don't know," I murmured. "I don't know." And I left her there, stuffing food into her ancient freezer.

When I got outside, I tried a deep breath. The night air was heavy with exhaust fumes. I couldn't get my lungs to expand.

At the phone booth on the corner I stuck in a dime and punched my home number. I got Roz.

"Is she there?"

"No."

"Have you heard from her?"

"Nothing."

"Well, get the hell out and look for her."

I hung up and got through to Mooney after letting the damn thing ring about fifty times.

"Got anything?" I asked him.

"The lawyer's here. And I've got Canfield, but he won't say squat till he talks to his attorney. We're gonna host a goddamn meeting of the American Fucking Bar Association."

I told him Marta knew zip, and I asked him to put out an all-points for Paulina.

I knew I ought to go home, the way a child lost in the woods knows he ought to stay put and wait for the search party. But what if the familiar path is right over the hill? What if the dark starts closing in and the rustling branches threaten?

What if Paolina was close at hand, somewhere I might find her?

Staying put is too damn hard.

I told myself she was okay. She'd taken care of herself last night, and she was smart enough to take care of herself tonight. I was less than convincing.

With the all-points, every cop in the metro area would be looking out for her. So what the hell did I think I could add? One more pair of searching eyes. A knowledge of her habits.

As I drove, my eyes peered into the shadows. Just because Paolina had been at Hunneman, I lectured myself, just because she had spoken to the woman who'd called herself Manuela, given her my business card, was no reason to believe she was mixed up in this mess any further. Her disappearance was her own idea, triggered by Marta's angry words.

I drove through Harvard Square, where one more young runaway would hardly be noticed, staring in the doorways where the musicians played on summer weekends, searching the sheltered depths of Holyoke Center, stopping to get a good look at the clutches of leather-clad youngsters.

Bands of young kids roamed the Cambridge Common. I abandoned the car and trailed a pack of them on foot, showed them a photo of Paolina, managed not to hit any of them when they sneered. I drew a ragged girl aside. She couldn't have been more than fourteen. She wore a thin suede jacket, fashionably fringed and frayed, scant protection against the coming winter. For five dollars she really looked at Paolina's picture. I believed her when she said she'd never seen her in the Square.

Hours later I found myself visiting the last-gasp places and realized I ought to quit. Paolina surely knew enough not to run to the Combat Zone, Boston's adult-entertainment district, Boston's sewer. But then, as Marta had said, what did I know?

I cruised Park Square near the bus terminal, looking for the ladies of the night, the sidewalk hostesses who might have noticed a young girl waiting for a bus. I flashed my photo of Paolina. Some of the women would have told me anything for a few dollars, but others said they'd never seen her, and I was relieved.

Where do you run when you're too young to have anywhere to run to?

Would she try to get back to Colombia? To learn more about this new father? The image of my own dad came back to me so strongly, I thought I could smell the cigar smoke. A cop, he'd smoked every day of his life, a three-pack-a-day man, plus those evening cigars. I quit right after he died of emphysema, his last days a hospital nightmare of tubes, shots, and pills. Oxygen masks. The painful struggle for breath.

212

How would I feel if I suddenly learned that he wasn't my father? Me, the daughter who'd become a cop in his image? It would be like an earthquake, I thought. Something I'd always counted on would have moved, altered irrevocably. The very earth would seem treacherous.

Paolina's brothers would have become her half brothers in a moment's revelation.

I debated a trip to the airport, gave it up, drove home with my heart tight in my chest. I imagined her at my front door, sleepily greeting me when I arrived. She wasn't there.

I fell asleep as the sun was starting to rise, a quarter to six. Two hours later I woke, filled with an urgency that seemed almost an extension of a dream.

I called Mooney and argued with him until he agreed to meet me in half an hour at a doughnut shop near the apartment on Westland Avenue.

34

I got there first and perched on a stool at the dingy counter. A lone waitress who looked like she'd been working three nights straight reluctantly plodded by. I ordered a large coffee with cream and two sugars in case she fell asleep before getting back to me. She swabbed the grimy countertop in front of me with a piece of rag even dirtier than the Formica. She kept staring at the door, waiting for her relief to come in, sighing and yawning for the benefit of the guy behind the cash register. Husband, maybe. She slopped some of my coffee into the saucer when she plunked it in front of me. I ordered two glazed doughnuts, my favorites. They tasted like sweetened, gluey paper.

Mooncy was eighteen minutes late. The waitress's replacement still hadn't shown up. She took a break from glaring at the wall clock, slammed down a coffee cup, and snarled at him while she took his order for Danish.

He downed a gulp and shuddered. "Don't you start, too, Carlotta," he warned before I got a word out. I have seen Mooney in many different guises, from spit-and-polish dress uniform to undercover sleaze, but I've seldom seen him look worse. His eyes had dark smudges beneath them, and there was stubble on his chin.

"I know you're late for a good reason," I said de-

215

murely, resting my chin in my hand and batting my eyelashes up at him.

"Don't start. This Canfield thing is driving me crazy. I sent a uniform over to City Hall to check out marriage licenses, birth certificates, and all that crap, and it looks like your Lydia Canfield, wife of James Hunneman, the woman who owns part of the pillow factory, is my Harold Canfield's only sister. Which makes Hunneman Canfield's brother-in-law, and keeps the whole mess in the family. Earn a little money at Hunneman's factory, spend it on rent at Canfield's apartment. We brought Harold in, and damned if I didn't think he'd spill everything, what with us knowing the connection between him and Hunneman, but the bastard's just yanking our chains."

I drank coffee. It had probably been in the pot longer than the surly waitress had been on duty. "He stalling for a deal?"

"If he killed those women, or he knows who the hell did, I don't want him cutting any deal that's gonna keep his ass out of a cell—"

"But if that's the only way to find out—"

"Don't start," he said, chewing a lump of Danish. "Paolina home?"

"I've got Roz looking for her. Phoned Gloria, and she's going to have the cabbies keep an eye out. At first I thought it was just a fight with her mother . . ."

Mooney tried unsuccessfully to smother a yawn. "It's never just one damn thing." He downed more coffee like it was needed medicine. "Carlotta, it's always a pleasure to see you, but why am I eating Danish here instead of at my desk?"

"Listen, Mooney, I've been running through Ana's story in my mind all night. She denies knowing who I am. That's lie number one. You saw her reaction to me. And she hadn't been told my name or anything. She knew me. So I started thinking: When did she see me, when could she see me? I told you I saw Manuela, my client, the woman I thought was Manuela, speed away in an old clunker. I asked Ana if she drove a car. Remember what she said?"

"Something about not having a license."

"Right. She evaded the question."

"Okay," Mooney said. "So she could have been driving, could have seen you then. So what?"

"Let's go on to lie number two. She said she went back to Westland Avenue, took the risk of being picked up by Immigration, because *maybe* she left *something* in the room. Now that's a big lie."

"You think she had a more pressing reason to go back."

"Damn straight I do. The third thing that's bothering me is the money. The woman with the filigree ring left five hundred-dollar bills on my desk. Ana identified the ring as belonging to one of the women who roomed with her at Westland. Where's a woman like that going to get a hundred-dollar bill?"

Mooney chewed a bite of apricot Danish. It sounded stale.

"Who searched the Westland apartment, Mooney?"

"Competent detectives."

"Did they take it apart, really look for something somebody might have hidden there, hidden carefully?"

"Like a cache of hundred-dollar bills?"

"Yeah. Like that."

Mooney sighed. "So that's what I'm doing here. You want to check out that apartment."

"If Ana wanted to go back there so much that she risked *La Migra* picking her up, I want to know why."

217

"Me too." Mooney gulped the rest of his coffee and stood up, leaving more than half the Danish on his plate. I thought about snitching it, since the two gluey doughnuts hadn't done much to take the edge off, but its appearance was less than tempting.

"On me," I said, but Mooney was already halfway to the pay phone by the door. I shoved bills at the man behind the register, left a bigger tip than the waitress deserved.

"Dave'll meet us with the key," Mooney said when I caught up to him.

35

The door to the basement apartment was sealed with official Boston Police Department tape. Mooney slashed it as soon as he heard Dave's footsteps. Dave nodded at me in greeting, handed over the key. He looked almost as tired as Mooney. He hadn't shaved.

"Canfield say anything?" Mooney asked.

"Not to us," Dave replied.

I let the men enter first, took a deep breath, and followed. It was as bad as I'd remembered, maybe worse, what with the residue of the fingerprint boys and the search team.

I said, "Too bad you can't put Canfield away for renting a rat hole like this."

Dave nodded agreement. Mooney said, "Where you wanna start?"

Dave said, "The guys went through here—"

"I'm looking for a place you'd hide a wad of bills," I said, heading into the tiny back bedroom. I stopped short when I entered. The bloody mattress had turned rusty brown.

"If you want the bedroom, I'll take the—what do you call it?—kitchenette," Mooney yelled. "Dave, take the living room, okay? Maybe there's a stash in a couch pillow."

The burglar's rule of thumb is that women keep pre-

219

cious belongings as close to the bed as possible, jewelry under the mattress and stuff. That's why I wanted the bedroom. There was nothing under these mattresses but metal frames.

I didn't think of it right away. I had to go through all the other places in the room first, from the crucifix on the wall to the pseudo closet, before my eyes were drawn back to the mattresses.

They were no more than three inches thick, ill supported on iron frames, even thinner in the middle where the outline of many a sleeper remained. My spine ached at the sight of them. I yanked the mattress from the farthest bed, stood it on end, and began a more detailed examination.

The covering had once been white. Now it was somewhere between gray and beige, stained in ways I didn't want to think about. It smelled ripe.

Nothing on the front side of the first mattress. I flipped it over and started my examination of the back, trying to imagine where I'd attack a mattress if I wanted to hide something in it. Maybe the sides . . .

Nothing.

I could hear the rumble of activity from the other room. Mooney coughed. He was probably sifting through the flour and cornflakes.

I stood the second mattress on end, started the process over. I left the bloody one for last. Along the edge of the rusty, bloodstained mattress was the outline of a faint triangular scar. The stitching that closed the wound was fine and regular.

"Bingo!" I yelled, my voice too big for the room. I wondered if the upstairs tenants heard. The men in the next room did. They came running.

"Knife?" I have one in my handbag, a neat Swiss

220

Army affair with a corkscrew and everything. I thought either of the guys might have a bigger one.

Mooney's was strapped to his shin. He slipped it out with a sheepish glance at Dave. I'm not sure if the blade was under the legal three inches. I slit the mattress cover, plunged my hand in the opening, and removed a fistful of sticky padding. The blood had soaked through.

"Want me to—" Both Mooney and Dave must have seen the look of distaste that crossed my face.

"I'll do it," I snapped. I used to watch myself a lot more when I was a cop. No outward squeamishness back then, not with the boys observing.

I yanked out another handful of stuffing. "I'll try for a while, then you can take over. I won't hog all the action," I promised.

"What're you looking for?" Dave asked.

Mooney said, "Cockroaches, what do you think?"

"Thanks," I said, wrinkling up my nose and noticing gratefully that doing so no longer hurt. "That's all I need, a handful of roaches."

"Want a glove?" Dave asked helpfully. "Whatever you find might have prints."

I quickly yanked my hand out and accepted his offer. He handed me a thin plastic glove, the kind doctors use, not the black leather mitt I'd been expecting. Preparedness in the age of AIDS.

I scooped stuffing, wedging my arm farther and farther into the hole, wiggling it through all the way past my elbow. I felt a hard, thin ridge against my hand, wondered fleetingly if I'd finally found evidence of either coil or spring. "I think there's something," I muttered. I had to remove about six more handfuls of gunk before I could get a purchase on it. Thin and hard, like a laminated card. Bigger than a green card.

"Slash the opening a little wider," I said to Mooney.

"Get your arm out of the way."

"I trust you." I didn't want to let go of whatever it was I'd grabbed on to.

Mooney carefully enlarged the slit.

"Okay," I said. I slid out my hand, holding a grimy, brown leather folder. Mooney grabbed it, his hands encased like mine. I wondered where the cops got all the gloves.

The folder looked familiar. I knew where I'd seen two like it recently. "INS credentials," I said.

Mooney opened it and I stared at Harry Clinton's picture, at his name and the numbers and letters that seemed so official. Two hundred-dollar bills were neatly folded inside.

"Who the hell—?"

"Jamieson's buddy," I said flatly. "The one who told me about the undercover operation at Hunneman."

"Shit," Mooney said. He handed the folder to Dave. "Get this to prints right away, and then get it back to me. And get an APB out for this guy. I'll get Jamieson on the wire as soon as I get to the car. Carlotta . . ."

"Yeah?"

"Let's go talk to Ana."

36

Ana was in Interrogation Two, the room where I'd viewed
the videotape of my dead client, closeted with Marian Rutledge, the classy Harvard lawyer. Mooney stopped at the
coffee machine and bought himself a cup before hammer-
ing on the door. He knew better than to ask me if I wanted
cop-house coffee.

The lawyer opened the door, clad in a tailored gray
suit. "Good," she said curtly upon seeing the two of us.
"My client would like to speak to you."

Mooney raised an eyebrow. We went in and Ana
forced a shaky smile.

"We're not asking for any deal up front," Marian Rutledge said firmly. "But we are confident that our information will help your investigation, and if it does, a word on
Ana's behalf would be appreciated." She repeated the
same message for Ana's benefit, her Spanish as elegant as
her suit. Ana stared at her in openmouthed admiration.
Mooney was so tired, I wasn't sure he'd realized she was
female.

"She ready to make a statement?" he asked.

"Yes."

"I'd like a police translator, no offense to your Spanish."

"Fine," she said.

223

Mendez was summoned. Taping equipment was set up on the long rectangular table. Mooney checked to make sure it was in order.

The lawyer nodded to Ana when the machine began to hiss.

"¿Dónde comienzo?" Ana asked. Where do I begin?

Mooney said, "Begin with Manuela Estefan."

Ana looked at me, glanced at her lawyer, stared longingly at the battered wooden door. There weren't any windows, just dull beige walls. She took a deep breath. "We meet in the camp, in Texas. Brownsville, I think, is the name of the place. We tell each other stories, how we come, how we walk the long miles, how we leave our families and come here, and we are in the camp, and they say they will send us back, right back to El Salvador, we don't even get to stay a little while. There is barbed wire and it is crowded, many refugees like us, penned like animals. And a man comes to us, to me and Manuela and three others from my country, and he says he can help us, for money, for jewelry—or maybe for other things."

She blushed furiously and Marian Rutledge said, "Go on now, Ana."

"We are good girls," she declared. "Good girls. From poor families, yes, but we go to church. Good girls."

I thought I knew why she'd wanted me to stay in Mooney's office. Not me, in particular, but any woman.

I didn't think she'd talk any more with Mooney and Mendez in the room, not about that part of her story. She hesitated and swallowed a gulp of coffee. It went down the wrong way and she coughed.

"The man is a coyote, a guide," she continued. "Some he brings in from over the border, some he takes from the camps. He is a pig of a man, but he can do what he says, and soon we have bus tickets, and we come to this city, to

Boston together, and we have jobs at the factory and a place to stay. He promises papers, but they never come. At the factory they don't ask for papers."

"Go on, Ana," the lawyer prompted.

"More girls come to work, but the five of us are together. We work very hard for the promise of papers. Manuela, she complains, and they say if we complain, we go back to the camp, to Texas, back to El Salvador, even—back to die.

"For me it is enough. I have food to eat and I work for it, and nobody comes in the night to take me away. But Manuela, she knows more, she wants more. She talks about the other women she meets, the ones who have papers, and how they can live anyplace and do things, go out with young men and have children, families who grow up here.

"Manuela, she is the most clever of us. She finds out something, something I think about the man who is the coyote, a man we see sometimes at the factory when new girls come in. And soon Manuela has her green card. And she says to us that this secret is very valuable and it will buy green cards for all of us, for all her friends. And we drink wine and celebrate, and then Manuela is gone."

The recorder hummed. Mendez repeated every word, his voice calm.

"The women at the factory, they say Manuela sleeps with somebody to get her card, and then she goes off because she doesn't have to stay in such a bad place to work for so little money. But Manuela, she is so smart. She knows something. And the four of us, we think she will send for us, she will get us the green cards because she says she will, and she is not a woman who forgets.

"We wait for her, but we don't hear. Aurelia is the bravest of us—"

225

"Aurelia Gaitan," Mooney murmured.

"*Sí*. And she goes finally to the coyote after we wait many weeks. I think she maybe knows what Manuela knew, but she doesn't tell us. Maybe because another girl moves into the apartment and we don't know her so well, maybe—I don't know why. But soon the boss at the factory tells us he has a green card for Aurelia, and she has gone also, with Manuela, to work somewhere wonderful, to California where it's warm always, and we are happy for her, but sad, puzzled she did not say good-bye.

"We wish, the three of us, very much that Manuela had told us the secret that buys the green cards, and at home when the new girls are out, we decide to look everywhere in the apartment because Manuela is tricky and maybe she hides things and that is how Aurelia knows how to get her papers and be North American and free."

Her coffee cup was empty. Mendez went out and got her a refill. She sipped it gratefully.

"In the mattress of Manuela's bed, where a new girl is sleeping, we find it. The card you show me, Manuela's green card, and much money, and suddenly everything is upside down. Because why would Manuela go away to work in California and leave her green card, which she is so happy about and so proud, and she will need wherever she goes in this country? Why would she leave this money, and where does this money come from? I am very afraid she is in jail.

"Delores says she will ask the man, the coyote, about the card. Maybe, she thinks, there are two cards, one—*¿cómo se dice?*—temporary, one for real."

"And Delores went away," I said. And of course the other two couldn't go to the police, wouldn't dream of it. Where do you turn when you grow up in a country where uniformed men haul people away in the dead of night?

When any cry for help in your new country could boomerang and bring deportation?

Ana nodded bleakly and rubbed her arms, as if she were suddenly chilled. "That leaves only Amalia and myself. We are younger than the others. We decide that we do nothing until we hear from one of the women. They will not leave us without a word. We go to work, we are very quiet, we don't complain, even when they have us work more hours. We have no secret to tell, so we don't complain. We have no place to go and our friends are gone. And then two things happen quick together.

"We hear about you." She nodded in my direction. "Someone who is not the police, a woman like us, and then we hear a woman talk about Manuela and how they find her dead. It's so long, you understand, months, and in our hearts we see Manuela in California, working somewhere nice, selling dresses, maybe, with a boyfriend, maybe, and we don't know what is true. And Amalia buys a newspaper and has someone read her the story, and we don't know how to find out what really happened and we want the green card back, Manuela's green card, because we think maybe that is what Manuela hid for us, the thing that is so valuable. Maybe we . . . I don't know what we thought. Amalia is smarter than me. She says she will go to you. She will take the money we find with the green card—"

I broke in. "Why would Amalia tell me she was Manuela?"

"Because then you will get the card and ask no questions."

"But the picture—" I said.

"Manuela is her *prima,* her cousin. She looks a little like Manuela."

227

"But didn't you want to know who the dead woman was?"

"No," Ana said forcefully. "No. We know our friends are in California. Our friends. My friends . . ."

She started to cry in earnest now. "And then Amalia is gone and the boss at the factory says to me, don't worry, the ones who leave get their green cards, and I must move to a new apartment because the officials find the other place and they know the girls who stay there have no papers, but I don't know anymore, and I move in with somebody else and I do my work and I leave and walk around and I don't go near the boss and I'm afraid the next time the coyote comes back, he'll know that we went for help, that Amalia talked to this lady. And I think if I look some more in the old apartment, maybe Manuela left something else there, maybe deeper in the mattress. And I go. I am so stupid, I go. And instead a policeman is there."

She came to an abrupt halt and buried her face in her hands.

The knock on the door startled all of us. It made Ana cry out. Dave walked in and handed Mooney Clinton's ID folder. "A few partials," he said. "Should I have her take a look at it?"

"No!" Mooney said quickly. "Lift the photo out and get five more like it—cop photos, perps, whatever. We let her pick him out. We're doing this by the book. This bastard's not going to walk."

Ana picked him out of a group of six with no hesitation.

Son of a dog, she called him, and she spat.

37

Harrison Clinton, I said to myself as I piloted my car home from the station. Was I surprised? Numb? Shocked? Angry? Angry, yes, because I'd believed a man who had a set of credentials, a deferential drawl, a face and body that stood up to close scrutiny. Had attraction made me blind? Shouldn't I have questioned his distrust of Jamieson? Instead my own dislike of Jamieson made Clinton seem more reasonable.

Good old Harry Clinton. A man whose work might take him from Boston to Texas to Boston again, with no one asking too many questions about his comings and goings. . . . A man with access to any one of the boxy neutral sedans, the Arics, Reliants, and low-cost Chevys the INS kept as agency cars. A man who lied as easily as he breathed. "If I'd been tailing you, you wouldn't have known it, ma'am." I'd believed him.

A man who'd kissed me. To be honest, a man I'd kissed. A man I'd almost invited to bed. A man who extorted and raped and killed. I sucked in air and sped through the tail end of a yellow light.

I should have— I stopped myself on the edge of a pit of self-recrimination. I know it's useless, but the habit clings.

The Toyota made the turn into my driveway of its

own accord. I rummaged in my handbag for keys. It took all my concentration to fit the key into the lock and make the door work.

I hollered for Roz, but there was no answering yell. Still out looking for Paolina. I thought about joining the search, but I knew damn well I needed a couple hours with the covers over my head before I could function.

I wrote Roz a note in bold red Magic Marker: "If you hear from Harry Clinton, wake me immediately! Don't trust him!"

I thought about adding another brief sentence. "He's a killer." Then I tried "He's a murderer." Either way Roz wouldn't believe me.

There was a note on the fridge reminding me not to miss tomorrow's volleyball practice. Biggest game of the season coming up. I took the note down and replaced it with my larger red warning. Then I checked the meager contents of the refrigerator, yanked out a carton of orange juice, and stood in the chill of the open door, gulping it down.

T. C. came yowling into the room, and I wondered when I'd last fed him. I fetched a can of his favorite FancyFeast and tried to make amends. He sneered at me, but he gobbled like a starved alleycat.

Barely managing to negotiate the stairs and kick my sneakers off, I fell asleep fully dressed, sprawled across the bedclothes. I woke a seeming instant later to the shrill demand of the telephone. My mouth felt dry as bone.

The voice was a familiar Texas drawl. I sat up in bed, suddenly alert and focused. My hand tightened on the receiver.

"Uh, hi," I said, willing my voice deliberately casual.

"I'm calling about Saturday night."

"Uh, yeah," I managed.

"Think you can make it? Dinner?"

"Sure," I said evenly. "Glad you remembered. Looking forward to it."

There was a long pause. I could hear him breathing. He gave a snort that might have been a laugh. "You know, you're good. Real good. Almost good enough."

"What do you mean?"

"Look, I know," he said. His voice was different, colder. The words came faster and the good-old-boy accent had diminished.

"What do you know?"

"You're the bitch who screwed it up. She'd never have gone to the cops on her own."

"Where are you?" I said.

The voice got lazy again. "You knew about me, didn't you? That's why you put me off. Otherwise we'd have gone upstairs and fucked, right? I never have trouble with women. I mean, I don't have to buy it or beg for it, you know."

I tried to picture Harry Clinton. This man on the phone had his voice, but it seemed to me, listening to him, that his appearance must have changed. How I hate it that monsters look normal. The deception of that outward normality prickled up my spine as I listened to him rant.

"I mean, I had to cut up Manuela, didn't I? Once I realized the stupid bitch didn't have the damned card on her. Somebody finds the card, matches it to the corpse, they're going to start checking Immigration files, right? Lead 'em to my little side business. You know, everything that happened, it's Manuela's damned fault. She stole my ID folder, stole it while she was doing me in the back room at Hunneman. Cutting her was bad, you know? She was okay, smart. Too smart. Like you. Are you listening to me?"

231

"Yeah," I said. "I'm listening."

"I had to kill those other women too. Can you believe that Manuela, telling all those other bitches about me? About where I worked and what my real name was? Cutting them was bad, but I cleaned it all up. I can think rings around any cop. Jamieson, he up and asked me about phony green cards. Hell, it *wasn't* phony, just blank. I did the photo for Manuela, to gain a little time. The damn blackmailing bitch. You listening?"

"Yes. Where are you?"

"You're gonna help me get out of this. There's no real evidence against me. I cleaned everything up. There's just that damned woman, the one the police have, thanks to you. She can say it's me, convince a jury. Other than her word they'll never get squat. I want her, and you're going to deliver her."

"Forget it. There's plenty of evidence. Once they start doing forensics with you in mind, they'll be able to—"

"Shut up. There's nothing a good lawyer can't knock down. I'm no moron. I'm a pro. I wanted to be a cop, you know that, but I got into this immigration stuff instead. I know all about forensics. But that woman, she gets all teary-eyed and a jury buys anything she says. Juries don't give a damn about fingerprints and expert testimony. But give 'em a victim, an eyewitness, and they slobber all over the floor. Hell, what am I talking trial for? There won't *be* a trial. I'm walking away from this. You're gonna help me. Help me get that Ana girl away from the cops. So listen."

"I've been listening."

"This part you might want to write down."

"What?"

"My terms."

"For giving yourself up?" I grabbed an old bank statement and a pencil from my bedside table while I spoke. I stared at my wristwatch, noted the time.

"Go ahead, play stupid. Go ahead. You don't need to understand. Just tell your cop friend I want to deal. I want that Spanish girl they've got in jail. I want her delivered to me today, this afternoon, at three o'clock. You'll escort her."

"Where?"

"I'll call back in an hour."

"The cops aren't going to go along with this stunt. Why the hell should they?"

"Well, I sure thought I was in trouble," he said as if he hadn't heard my question. "Jamieson sniffing around, you out at Hunneman's. Thought I might be in too deep, but I guess I'm a lucky man."

He made that noise again, the one that might have been a laugh. "I got me a guest in my office. You want to say hello to your baby sister? You hang on now, and I'll put her right on the line."

"Paolina?" I could barely get the name out.

"Carlotta," came her small, scared voice. "I'm sorry—"

"I'll be in touch," drawled Clinton. And the line went dead. I kept jiggling the little button and repeating her name.

38

"Mooney," I said urgently, moving forward in my seat until he had to meet my eyes or turn his face to avoid me, "I'm trusting you on this."

"Carlotta, the bastard isn't giving us a hell of a lot to work with." His voice was flat and lifeless. I remembered hearing it like that before, when he'd phoned the wife of a young cop wounded in action. His colorless monotone gave nothing away, surely not the deathbed gravity of the rookie's condition.

We were parked in an unmarked unit on Boston Common, outside the entryway to Park Street Station, largest and busiest of Boston's subway stations. Shoppers lined up for tokens at the outside booth; more swarmed down the steps to take places in another line inside. The newsstand vendors grabbed quarters and dispatched folded *Globe*s and open tabloid *Herald*s. The Fens serial killer was still front-page stuff. Hot-dog and balloon men sold their wares to hordes of tourists. Mooney was behind the wheel. I rode shotgun. Ana was in the backseat, sandwiched between Joanne Triola and a scowling Walter Jamieson.

Harry Clinton's call had come an endless ten minutes late. By that time Mooney was seated next to me at the kitchen table, the phone was tapped, and a horde of

235

headphoned technicians lurked outside in a phone-company truck, bent over high-tech consoles, trying to trace the call. It was a crazy long shot, but nobody wanted to let the chance to shake out the equipment go by.

"Keep him on the line," Walter Jamieson had urged when the phone finally sounded. He was sitting across from me at the table. I wasn't pleased about having him, but Mooney'd brought him along.

It was a dumb thing to say. I knew I was supposed to keep the creep talking.

I'd tried, but he wasn't in the mood. "Have the girl at Park Street Station, three this afternoon, first level outbound, where the C train loads. The station has to stay open. Any barricades, any construction work, anything unusual, the deal's off. You walk Ana in. No guns. No cops. You'll get instructions."

"Let me—"

He'd hung up and I'd finished saying "talk to Paolina" in my head.

His voice had been projected on a speaker, so I hadn't needed to repeat the message. He'd sounded brisk and efficient. None of the mania of the earlier call showed, none of the frayed nerves.

"Cool," Jamieson had observed. "Very much in control."

"If he was in control, he'd be gone," Mooney'd said. "This stunt is crazy. He'll never get away."

"He will if it's a choice between him and Paolina," I'd snapped. "I wish I'd stayed the hell out of this."

I wished I'd raced to the cops the minute I'd heard about the Hunneman plant. But I'd been afraid I'd lose Paolina, afraid Marta would carry out her threat and move away if the factory closed.

I might lose Paolina anyway, I thought.

"I'll remind you the next time." Mooney must have seen the look on my face. His voice petered out and he'd averted his eyes, staring at his wristwatch as if it had secrets written across the dial.

"Three o'clock. Right at the beginning of the Park Street rush," he'd commented gloomily. "We can rule out firepower. The commissioner gets flack for high-speed chases on deserted highways. He's not going to go for staging some *High Noon* shootout at Park Street Station."

"Clinton's one smart, crazy bastard," Jamieson had said admiringly.

"Maybe if you'd mentioned you suspected him—" I'd said.

"Maybe if you'd told us anything—"

"Shut up," Mooney had thundered. "We haven't got the time."

We didn't. We had less than three hours.

Mooney worked the telephone, notifying the INS and the FBI and the commissioner's office, bringing in only those who needed to know, only those he trusted most. A slow infiltration of the subway stop began—a vendor here, a cleaner there.

"Not too many cleaners," I protested. "He'll know they're phonies."

The rep from the MBTA looked up indignantly. Mooney placed a restraining hand on my arm.

Marta was at Lilia's. At first I hadn't wanted to tell her. What's the use? I'd said, bad news keeps. I'd almost felt she didn't deserve the truth, not after deceiving Paolina for so long. But she had a right to know, a mother's right to worry.

Mooney sent in people disguised as train conductors and token dispensers, but only at shift change or lunch break, only when the regular employee could be intercepted and fed some plausible lie about not being needed.

"He's smart," Jamieson kept saying. "Look what he's done so far."

"Right," I snapped.

"I don't mean the killings," he said quickly. "But the rest—that was neatly done, you got to admit. He must have made a mint bringing in aliens, collecting from them for the trip, then hitting up employers desperate for cheap labor, collecting for protection."

"He wasn't as smart as Manuela Estefan," I said defiantly.

But he was. He was alive. She was dead.

Jamieson cleared his throat. "Anyhow, what I meant to say is that he'll check out the area, go downstairs, wait for a few trains, see if everything's running right. Anything out of the ordinary, he's gone."

And the beauty of Park Street as a switch point was that he could go just about anywhere. Down to the lower level and out through any one of half a dozen exits. Onto his choice of Green Line or Red Line trains. Inbound, outbound. Through tunnels, up steps, across tracks.

"Carlotta," Mooney said at about a quarter to three, startling me out of my trance, "take Ana for a little walk. Back in ten minutes."

"Huh?"

"He could be out there now. Here on the Common. I want him to see her with you. You can test the wire."

I shrugged. It didn't make much sense to me, but I was itchy from the enforced idleness of the car, willing to do anything to stretch my legs.

"We may take off, but we'll be back here in ten," Mooney promised. "Don't go downstairs until you check in with me."

Ana and I got out and walked toward the Park Street fountain. The brass basin was dry, the way it is most of the year, with the carved fishes gasping their surprise instead of spouting water. A raincoated man with a wireless mike called sinners to repent for the love of sweet Jesus Christ. Nobody paid him any more attention than they'd pay a strolling violinist in a crowded restaurant.

I wondered for the seventeenth time about a gun. I'd decided not to take one. Because I was afraid I'd use it. A subway station is no place for guns. If I had one, I might rely on it. I might lose my self-control, endanger Paolina —I knew all the goddamned reasons, and my hand still ached for a weapon.

"You okay?" I asked Ana. Dumb question. I asked it to see if the techs could pick up what I was saying.

"Sí."

The man she feared most in the world was waiting down in the guts of the station for her. Sure, she was okay.

The wire worked fine above ground. It was underground that static ruled. Mooney said it might work. It was worth the chance.

It wasn't worth wiring Ana. It would just make killing and dumping her quickly more attractive to Clinton. So it was up to me to keep the cops informed while convincing Clinton the cops were nowhere around.

On the main path across the Common, two tall black guys ran the regular three-card monte scam. The faces changed from year to year, the game remained the same. I did a quick crowd scan, picked out the shill in maybe ten seconds. He glanced up and recognized me from my cop days, grinned hesitantly, relaxed as I strolled on by.

We retraced our steps and circled the fountain twice. The sky was clear blue broken by wisps of cirrus. The church steeple was dazzlingly white. All the sounds seemed muted, separate. I felt like I was walking in fog, like no one could see me. People rushed by and I wondered if anyone could read the horrors in my mind. I wondered if Harry Clinton could see us, perched somewhere in the distance, eyes glued to binoculars. I wondered which of the hot-dog vendors was a cop.

I wondered where the wire techs were. No telephone trucks. Clinton would have been on to that in a flash.

The car pulled up in front of us. I put a cold hand on Ana's arm and without another word we walked toward it. I got in the front door. Ana got in the back.

"Madre de Dios," she muttered, inhaling sharply.

Jamieson was no longer in the backseat. Instead there sat a woman who could have been Ana's twin. Her sister, at least, I thought, staring at her more closely.

"What the hell?" I said to Mooney. "Oh, no, this isn't going to—"

"Carlotta." It was Joanne Triola talking now. "This is Sergeant Ramirez, on loan from Lowell. We weren't sure we could get her here in time. She's undercover Narcotics."

She was wearing the same green blouse, the same rust-colored skirt. Ana was removing her raincoat, handing it over.

"Her height and weight are almost the same. She's wearing a wig. No way is Clinton going to spot the substitution."

"Mooney," I protested, "you promised. Nothing funny until Paolina's away."

"I can't give him Ana," Mooney said.

"Mooney—"

"He needs distance, Carlotta. To get away. He's not going to get close to you. It's too goddamn dangerous for

240

him. From a distance she's perfect. Just keep the bastard at a distance."

"Yeah, but . . ." I began, thinking of a hundred, a thousand, a million things that could blow up in my face, in Paolina's face.

"It's time."

"Goddammit, you could have told me before. You should have said—"

"What good would it have done, Carlotta?" Joanne chimed in. "This is the way it's going to be."

Ana was staring at her look-alike, her savior. The two of them rattled away in Spanish. Ana's eyes lost their haunted look.

Mooney said, "You okay, Ramirez?"

"Ready."

The church clock tolled three.

"You're on," Mooney said.

The two of us got out of the car. Me from the front seat, her from the rear. Just like last time. Except different.

We waited in line, bought our tokens, went downstairs. Ramirez huddled into Ana's raincoat.

I blinked, heading from the bright daylight into the artificial cave. The stairs were jammed with people and I kept my gaze on those closest. I didn't want Clinton edging up to me before I was ready, seeing the fake Ana. How well had he known the woman? God, if he'd had sex with her at that camp in Texas, I hoped he'd done it in the dark.

I stared at Ramirez. Ana's face was a little broader, younger. They both had round brown eyes. The hair was perfect.

We pushed through the turnstiles alongside shoppers hefting paper bags, students with backpacks, suited businessmen stealing an early march on the commuter crowds.

The C trains, heading outbound to Cleveland Circle, loaded on the right side of the main platform, halfway down, in front of a refreshment stand that sold newspapers, doughnuts, coffee, popcorn. I took a deep breath. The popcorn oil smelled rancid.

Ramirez and I took up a position in front of the stand. She turned automatically to face me. It was a good move, averting her face from the majority of the crowd. I wanted to ask her first name. It didn't seem like the time or place for small talk.

After eight minutes that felt like eight hours, a young black kid in a leather jacket came up to me and said, "You Carlotta?"

I nodded. He handed me a folded sheet of paper and ran off.

I read the typed instructions aloud. I didn't have much faith in the wire. The train noise was deafening. I could barely hear myself.

The note said, "You and the girl board the next train. Stand rear door right side. Both hands on pole. Don't talk to strangers. Get off at Arlington. Bring this message with you."

So much for crumpling the note and throwing it on the ground for one of Mooney's cleaners to find. If the wire wasn't working, nobody would know where we'd gone.

A young man was pushing a broom nearby. I said to Ramirez, "We're going to Arlington." The broom pusher didn't look up. I hoped he'd heard. I hoped he was one of Mooney's guys.

The next train was crowded. We had to push and shove our way on. An elderly lady glared at me as I shoved past her. I kept an arm on Ramirez's shoulder. We didn't speak. I wondered how much they'd had time to tell her.

More people piled on at Boylston. I was still busy examining the crowd that had boarded at Park and previous points. Clinton wasn't on the train, not standing up anyway. Maybe seated behind the barrier of torsos. Maybe in another car. Maybe already at Arlingon. I hoped so. Distance, keep him at a distance.

I thought of all the cleverly concealed cops watching the exits from Park Street. Would Mooney blow their cover and try to run them over to Arlington? How many exits were there from that station? Damn near as many. Four on the corner of Boylston and Arlington. Then there was the tunnel to Berkeley Street. And the trains.

We got off with a burst of others at Arlington, stood while the crowd rushed around us, some making for the exits, some piling onto the train. A hand touched me from behind. I whirled, saw nothing, heard a voice from the level of my waistline.

A small boy tugged at my shirt. "Man said give you this."

Again a sheet of paper. I read it aloud. If Clinton was watching, I hoped he'd think I was reading it to Ana.

" 'Look across the tracks.' "

I stopped, did. They were there. He had Paolina by the hand.

" 'Look across the tracks,' " I said again. " 'Walk up the staircase, stay at the top where I can see you. I'll send Paolina when you send the girl. Then go back down and get on first train.' "

Damn. I glanced to my left. The staircase loomed some sixty feet away. There was an identical staircase on Clinton's side of the tracks. Both led to the fare collector's

243

plaza, a concrete island the width of the subway tunnel. I remembered the setup at Arlington Street; the staircase landings were only forty feet apart. I stole a glance at Ramirez.

Why couldn't we pull the switch now, me sending the fake Ana up the stairs, him parting with Paolina at the same time?

I answered my own question. Because that way both Ana and Paolina would be out of sight for a few seconds during the crossover, because Ramirez could grab Paolina, take shelter in a fare collector's booth, run for an exit.

We started to walk toward the stairs. Ramirez stayed to my left. It looked natural, and I silently applauded her for keeping out of clear sight. But once upstairs, at forty feet, maybe less . . .

I wondered if Ramirez was armed, wired. Hell, I didn't know anything. Damn Mooney. Damn their convenient timing. The staircase seemed to stretch forever. I kept my eyes right, focused across the tracks where Clinton and Paolina were mimicking our movements. He had his hand in the pocket of his light jacket. The pocket bulged.

There was a very brief moment when we lost sight of each other. I said "Staircase, Arlington Street Station. Gun in jacket pocket" as fast and as loud as I could.

Then I could see him again. He clutched Paolina by the hand, yanking her along in front of him. He paused at the top of the steps and we faced each other across the span. Too close, I thought despairingly.

Someone jostled me from behind, snapped "Excuse me." Throngs of rushing homeward-bound commuters tried to shove Ramirez and me aside. I didn't want to take any more steps forward. I grabbed the fake Ana and we dodged to the left. The station was dense with people. I stared across the too-narrow gulf and saw that Clinton was having as much trouble as I was with the shoving, rushing pedestrians. He was trying to keep a firm grip on Paolina, on the gun in his pocket, and still get a clear view of Ana. I could see him easily, but then we were both taller than the crowd. Paolina was practically invisible. Ana must have been nearly as hard to see.

I held my breath.

The noise level increased threefold as a rush of local high-school kids, freed from class, poured down the stairs and through the turnstiles, waving their T passes, moving to deafening rap music from a red-lining boom box. Instead of neatly splitting between the two staircases, heading inbound or outbound, they stood mid-platform, arguing and gesturing, finishing off some school dispute.

I could barely see Clinton. I heard him shout. Then I saw Paolina twisting and weaving through the crowd. Clinton yanked something from his pocket and I yelled "Down!" I hollered at full volume, with desperation behind the shout, but my voice was lost in the uproar.

Paolina was a just a flash between somebody's legs, trying to push her way through to me. I could see that her mouth was open, but I couldn't tell if she was screaming or what she was screaming. Clinton raised his weapon. He wasn't sighting on Paolina. I turned and knocked Ramirez to the ground.

The first shot brought silence, the second panic. Paolina was in front of me, her arms wrapped around me, almost knocking me over. I whirled and thrust her behind me, pushing her down two steps behind a cement barrier.

"Stay here," I yelled. "Let go."

I stood and surveyed chaos. One of the schoolkids was down. I couldn't see Ramirez. Clinton turned, stuffed his gun back in his pocket, joined the race downstairs. Bewildered commuters stood and screamed. Guards in MBTA uniform swarmed and shouted. I caught a glimpse of Ramirez hauling herself to her feet. There was blood high on the shoulder of Ana's raincoat. She had a gun in her hand. She sank back on the ground. I yelled, "Officer down! Officer in need of assistance!" as loudly as I could, praying somebody was picking up something from the damn machine strapped tight to my ribs. Then I pushed in close to her, grabbed the gun from her unresisting hand, and plunged through the crowd, down the staircase, after Harry Clinton.

"Get down! Get out of the way!" The stolid citizens on the staircase had no eyes, no ears. They hadn't heard shots, just backfires, hadn't seen anything out of the ordinary, just a guy racing to catch some train. Damn inconsiderate of people, rushing around, shoving on a staircase. Somebody could get hurt, dammit.

I kept the automatic at my side, pointed at the ground, invisible. Ramirez had already clicked the safety off. From ten steps up I surveyed the station platform. It was a blur, a whirl of shapes and colors. My eyes picked out bits of movement. A boy grabbed his father's hand. A flash of red turned into a young woman's scarf. Blue was a book bag, an umbrella. Most of the faces were in profile or turned three-quarters away, gazing down the tunnel for the headlight of the train. Where was he? Racing for the Berkeley Street exit? On a train back to Park Street? Behind a pillar? My breath was coming in starts and stops. The train rumble hammered my ears. My hand shook. I wanted to shoot the bastard, kill him. Shoot bullet after bullet into his dying body, yelling their names, Manuela, Aurelia, Delores, Amalia—

An Arborway–Huntington train lurched into the station. I watched the doors part, spilling new innocents onto the platform. I knew if I saw Clinton, I'd never get a clear shot off. I'd hit some poor kid reaching for his father's hand.

I remembered Ramirez, bleeding on the ground. And the anonymous kid who'd fallen. And Paolina, crouched on the staircase, vulnerable.

I swallowed and shoved the safety on the automatic. My mouth tasted like metal. I crammed the gun in my pocket, turned, and raced back up the stairs, making myself small against the banister, pushing against the crowd every step of the way. The sound of approaching sirens added to the cacophony.

Paolina was where I'd left her, eyes wide and staring. A gray-haired woman was trying to comfort her, but Paolina was deaf to her soothing words. She moaned softly. I knelt in front of her, called her name. Her eyes focused slowly on my face, and then she was in my arms. I picked her up, and it seemed as if she had no weight. She crushed the transmitter into my ribs and the pain felt good.

39

At eight-thirty the next morning, dressed in shorts and long-sleeved top, I was resting my butt on the hard wooden bench of the Huntington Avenue Y's gym, listening to the smack of sneakers on floorboards, the referee's shrill whistle, sporadic yells, and brief bursts of applause. Mainly I heard the cheers of the rival squad. We were down a game.

And I was decorating the bench.

My nose and cheekbone were fine. An ice pack wrapped my left ankle, more or less secured with an Ace bandage. I'd played only the opening two points. I must have slipped on the damn staircase at Arlington Street station, maybe when I'd lifted Paolina. I hadn't noticed the pain, not till this morning.

Kristy had given me a long look when I'd limped in. Ordinarily I hate missing a practice, much less a match— and this was the championship, and here I sat on the bench. I stretched out a hand and rested it on Paolina's knee. She turned and gave me a tentative smile.

"Maybe you can go back in," she said earnestly. I reached over and tucked a strand of shiny hair behind her ear so I could see her better.

"Maybe."

"I'm sorry you hurt your ankle."

"It's not your fault."

Her hand crept into mine. She was okay. A bruise or two, hidden by her striped shirt. A scraped knee under blue-green pants. Her fingers toyed with a goldfish pendant, suspended on a black silk cord, the twin of the one I'd found in my house. She was physically okay, but much, much too quiet.

While I was changing in the locker room pretty Edna had asked about handsome Harry, the Olympic scout. Would he be watching today's game, cheering for me?

I hadn't told her Harry Clinton was locked in a cell at Charles Street Jail. The wire hadn't worked well on the station platforms. Too far underground. But Mooney had gotten the message to move to Arlington from the broom man at Park Street. And up on the staircase in Arlington, only ten feet beneath the street, my voice had carried loud and true. Harry Clinton had emerged at Berkeley Street to the hostile stares of six cops and two FBI men. With no hostage in tow.

He wasn't talking about the killings, not to the cops at least, except to say that they must be the work of a crazy man, and since he wasn't crazy, he couldn't be the murderer. Not crazy. This from a man who'd chopped off Manuela's hands to prevent her identification, and then repeated the pattern so the later deaths would seem like the work of a ritualistic killer who chose his victims at random.

Smart didn't rule out crazy.

Ramirez was in Boston City Hospital with a broken collarbone. The kid who'd gone down had a shattered kneecap.

"It's just I thought I saw him today," Edna said, double-tying her shoelaces, a puzzled frown creasing her brow.

250

I wondered if she'd ever link the Olympic scout with the mug shots of Harry Clinton on the front pages of both dailies.

James Hunneman was at police headquarters, practically stuttering in his eagerness to talk. The factory owner swore he didn't know a damn thing about murder. He was only bribing Clinton. It had been going on for a long time.

He'd always gotten cheap labor from Clinton, no questions, no papers, dollars changing hands. When the new law took effect, making him vulnerable to fines for employing illegals, he'd started paying Clinton more, to avoid INS raids. He made ends meet by sticking some of the illegals in his brother-in-law's rental apartments on Westland. Canfield charged what the traffic would bear and kicked back a percentage to Hunneman. Still, Hunneman thought it was getting out of hand. He could barely make a profit. American workers wanted more and more. Unions and benefits. Health care, for chrissake.

Hunneman's lawyer tried to get him to shut up at this point, but he was a man with a grievance and he wanted to set the record straight.

And Manuela, and the other women who so suddenly disappeared after supposedly getting their green cards?

Well, he blustered, he wasn't in business to ask questions. He didn't give a damn. They were just a bunch of illegals.

I hoped he'd see the inside of prison for a long time to come, he and his brother-in-law both. It wasn't enough. If there was a hell, I wanted them booked for an endless shift, stitching and stuffing pillows in a sweltering, unventilated closet.

The people in the stands came alive as Kristy made a terrific dig, and my replacement, a black woman named Nina, spiked a kill. Fourth game even at eight all. I yelled

251

encouragement. It felt funny to watch. The perspective was wrong.

"I'm all mixed up in my head," Paolina mumbled, leaning against me.

"Let's talk about it."

"Not now. You wanna watch."

"We'll take a walk. I'll test my ankle."

I leaned over and murmured to a teammate. If everybody else broke a leg, she could find me wandering the first-floor corridors. I took Paolina by the hand and we went out the big double doors. The noise of the game receded behind us.

"What's all mixed up in your head?" I asked after we'd walked awhile in silence. The ice bag thumped against my ankle.

"Does your ankle hurt?"

"Only when I tap-dance."

"Mom said not to tell you about the factory."

"Is that what's bothering you?"

"I gave Amalia your card. She was in the bathroom, crying, and she said no one could help her. I remembered how I always used to cry when I was a little girl, and I said maybe you could help her like you helped me."

When she was a little girl. When had a ten-year-old ceased being a little girl?

"I wish I could have helped her," I said. "She didn't tell me enough."

Paolina said, "She was crying. I hate it when grown-ups cry."

We were near a staircase, and I sat heavily on the third step up. I leaned forward and probed my swollen ankle with tentative fingers.

"If she'd told the truth," Paolina said hesitantly,

"would you have helped her? No matter who she was? No matter if she was illegal and everything?"

"I'd have done my best. I might not have helped, but I'd have tried."

"What if—what if she had a secret that was too awful to share?"

"Sometimes if you tell secrets, they don't seem so bad," I said.

She twisted the wire fish that dangled around her neck, ran her fingers over the black silk cord. "Mom lied to me," she said, "about my dad."

"Tell me about it," I murmured, almost afraid to talk for fear she'd shut me out again.

She went on and I breathed a little easier. "I just wanted to tell the truth and not hurt anybody."

"That's tough," I said. "Sometimes you can't tell the truth and not hurt somebody."

"I thought if I went to—to that man, he could help me because he worked for Immigration and everything, and because you liked him. I thought he was okay."

She stared at the floor. Her fingers were busy with the fish again.

"You saw him the night you stayed at my house with Roz. You took his card off the hall table."

"You kissed him," she said accusingly.

This was not the time for a lecture about spying from staircases. "I thought he was okay too. I made a mistake about him." I said gently, "The good guys don't wear white hats and the bad guys don't wear black."

"But then how can you tell?" she asked.

My mother always told me I couldn't trust anyone. She had a hundred ways to say it, couched in her own mother's useful Yiddish phrases. There were so many, all about the uselessness of strangers. The one that summed

253

it up was, *A goy blayht a goy.* A stranger remains a stranger. A Gentile is always a Gentile.

If you trust people, you could wind up bedding Harry Clinton.

Or loving Paolina.

She wasn't crying, but it cost her a gallant effort not to cry, and I wanted to tell her to let go, not to put on any brave front for me.

"Why did you need to talk to the Immigration man?" I asked.

She took a deep breath and continued in a shaky voice. "Because I'm illegal. I'm not an American."

"Oh, Paolina." I rested my hand on her head. Her shiny hair felt soft.

"My dad isn't from Puerto Rico. He's somebody I never met. I don't even have a picture of him. I never heard of him until we went to Bogotá."

"How did you find out?" I asked. I wanted to probe to the bottom of the wound, to make sure she talked it all out. But I kept my voice gentle and easy.

"We stayed with my aunt," she said, "my *tía* Rosa, but one night we went to this big house, this enormous house on the top of a hill. A woman in a uniform, like a nurse, answered the bell, and Mom said I should go with her. She took me down a long hallway, lit with candles, to the kitchen, and we had mint tea and cookies. She told me how to get to the bathroom, but I got lost. Maybe I took the wrong staircase. It was such a big house."

"Go on, honey."

"I kept walking around, looking at things. There was a big blue-and-yellow parrot on a stand in one hallway, and I talked to him but he didn't talk back. I kept thinking I'd find the kitchen again, and then I was on this balcony, in a tiny room that looked over another room, a room

254

with almost as many books as a library. And I heard my mom talking. I should have yelled down to her. But I didn't. I listened.

"She was talking to this old man. He had white hair and he was dressed all in black. She called him my grandfather, but he wasn't her dad, because I've seen pictures of Mom's dad in the scrapbooks. And I couldn't figure it out, so I stayed and listened to everything they said.

"They had a terrible fight. Mom wanted money. She said he owed it to me. And he called her names and said maybe I wasn't his granddaughter. And even if I was, he hated his son and he wouldn't give her any money. And later I asked Mom questions about the old man and whether he had any children because I thought maybe my real dad was dead or something."

How could Marta have been so foolish as to imagine Paolina didn't know?

"Is he dead?" I asked.

"I wish he was. I wish I never knew about him."

I could hear distant cheering from the gym, but I didn't connect the sound to volleyball. I didn't even wonder who'd won the fourth game.

Paolina said, "I pretended I was like you, like a detective. I asked my cousins and other people down there."

"And what did you find out?" I asked.

She bit her lip and tugged at her necklace. Then she said, "My father, my real father, is named Carlos Roldan Gonzales. He's one of those guys you read about in the papers with all the drugs. He used to just be a Communist or something, but now he's mixed up with drugs, and the police and the army chase him all the time, and everybody wants to kill him. Everybody hates him, and that's who my father is.

"Mom didn't even tell me. She let me think Dad was

255

my father, and he's not. I don't think he adopted me or anything. I'm not American, even. I'm like the women at the factory. I don't know who I am."

Her shoulders heaved and the tears started. At first she tried to stop them, sniffing them back, then she gave it up and cried like the small child she was, with grief and abandon.

"Paolina, honey, listen to me." I waited until she looked me in the eye. I should have given her a tissue. I never carry tissues when I need them. "You're the same person you were."

"No I'm not. I'm not the same. Look at me in school. Will everybody have to know? Will I get deported? Will I have to live with my father? I thought that man would know because he worked for Immigration, but he didn't care about anything except that I saw him at the factory."

"You're not going away. You won't get deported."

"Why? How?"

"We'll have to think about it and find out what's really true and what isn't. There are a lot of things we can do once we find out the truth."

"But—"

"Listen, the important thing is that you know who you are. You play drums in the band. You're my little sister. You're not your mother and you're not your father."

"But I'm like my mother. Lilia says I look like my mother."

"So you think you have to be like your father too?"

"I guess, but I don't want to be bad."

"Oh, Paolina." I stared at the floor and the ceiling and the walls and tried to find the words that would make it better. I touched the tiny gold fish on the black silky cord.

"Remember the fish," I said slowly. "How I thought it was a little stick man and you told me it was a fish. Well, to some people it's more than a fish. It's a symbol, a Christian symbol, a very old one. But it's something even more basic. It's gold wire twisted into a shape. Whether I think it's a fish or I think it's a man, it's still gold wire.

"What I'm trying to say is, you're you, whether you think you're different or not. Nothing has changed since you overheard that conversation except the way you think about yourself. You thought you were a gold fish because one man was your father. Now you think you're a stick man because somebody else is your father. But what you're made of is the same."

The swelling and the pain in my ankle seemed to decrease after that. I played eight minutes in the fifth and final game. I kept glancing over at Paolina, sitting on the bench, waiting for me. She had the very faintest of smiles on her face. We lost the game 15–12. It felt like a victory.